FROST MOON

BY PATRIK SAHLSTRØM

THE BOOKS OF FUTURE DARKNESS
VOLUME I

Published by:

NEW Productions AS
Ruseløkkveien 26
0251 Oslo
Norway

www.newpro.no

Cover illustration by Ragnhild Wisth;
Copyright © 2016 by NEW Productions AS

CreateSpace Print-on-Demand Paperback Edition
ISBN 978-82-93489-02-3

Thanks to those who made this book possible:

My dear family and parents, who believed in me,
even when it wasn't reasonable.

Niels E. Wisth, for editing and being god of all trades,
and his wonderful wife Ragnhild Wisth,
for the gorgeous cover.

And my esteemed test readers,
Fia Fjordholm,
Gaute Remman Gunnleiksrud,
and Lene Jacobsen.

PROLOGUE

In polite company, the weather would have been described as 'raining cats and dogs'. From Constansa's point of view, all the little felines and canines of heaven were pissing maliciously down on them. Her mood was foul; she hated babysitting. Mainly because whenever she was called to babysit anyone, it usually led to a major demon invasion and a few razed cities – not to mention the horrible death of the child in question. It just wasn't her forte.

The stench inside the limousine didn't exactly help either. The air conditioning might be state of the art, but that didn't help when it was choking on cigarette fumes. Constansa almost envied Katherine who was on point, scouting the monastery before the rest of them arrived. At least she was doing something. Constansa would have happily traded places with her; just sitting there drumming her fingers on the dashboard was a lot worse than being active and soaking wet out in the rain. Cullen was driving – badly – while Bartholomew and Theresa were trying to comfort their charge, Elisabeth. Fortunately, the limo had a flat screen TV and Theresa had had the foresight to pick up a bunch of children's DVDs to distract the kid. Ricardo was just lounging, filling the car with the smoke from his death sticks whenever he wasn't pretending to be asleep.

The child in question, Elisabeth, seemed like a sweet, polite, intelligent and pretty girl. Long dark curls and beautiful brown eyes were destined to make her man-eater – or woman-eater if she swung that way – once she got older. A couple of centuries ago, Constansa would have felt sorry for the kid. But those kinds of sentiments had received fatal wounds on the many battlefields where she'd fought. After all, the girl was alive, reasonably safe and healthy, and no one close to her had been tortured or murdered yet. Compared to the rest of the Multiverse, she had it good. Constansa remembered how Elisabeth had bravely told her parents that they shouldn't worry and that as long as she had her teddy bear Ursus along to protect her, she would be fine. The parents Constansa did feel sorry for. Here they were, happily striving to make a living and raise a happy family, when out of the blue it turned out that their daughter was a pawn in the game between Heaven and Hell and that she would be taken away to be raised in a convent. They weren't even told the name of the convent in question – for Elisabeth's safety. Constansa felt it would be safe to assume that at some point infernal forces would capture them and try to torture information on their daughter's whereabouts out of them.

At least Constansa's own parents had actually planned for her to join the war and were prepared for the price they had to pay – although it had to be admitted that they had expected their firstborn to be a boy. Back in Spain in the 15th century it had taken all of her family's wealth and political clout to give her a proper education. Her father was even crazy enough to host Arabic and Jewish scholars, risking the wrath of the Inquisition to make sure she was taught proper astronomy, philosophy, and medicine. It didn't pan out quite the way her parents had planned; after levelling parts of Lisbon during a fierce battle, in which Constansa lost control of her powers, she and Theresa were kicked out of their order and had to flee in shame across Europe, with the Inquisition hot on their heels. Compared to that, Elisabeth had it easy.

It was a shitty job anyway. If the soothsayers were to be believed, Elisabeth had the potential to be the most powerful magician of this age. The last time anyone of that caliber was around, he ended up nailed to a cross. And even if they managed to keep her safe for a while, it wasn't realistic that she should fare any better than the carpenter from Nazareth – whom according to people who had known him, back in the day, was a really nice guy. The only reason Constansa and her pack had ended up on babysitting duty was that they were equally despised by all factions of the Church. With Elisabeth under Constansa's protection, they were fairly sure Constansa wouldn't play favorites, and let Elisabeth choose her own way. Which was why this convent was chosen. Run by the Grey Friars, it was one of the few Church strongholds which had maintained strict neutrality during the schisms of the last few centuries – schisms that had brought the Church to its knees. Not that the Grey Friars were a particularly nice or friendly bunch – they were equal opportunity haters – but at least they produced mean Knights and Dames of Jesus and Constansa hoped that they would teach Elisabeth enough martial skills to keep her alive.

They had reached the small country road leading towards the convent. This was more or less the last chance for an ambush, so Constansa checked her weapons. Her shotgun was loaded with assorted silver, cold iron and blessed steel shrapnel and her sleek, razor-edged sword was within easy reach. Never having gotten around to trusting modern communication devices, she reached into her pocket and took out one of Bartholomew's communication crystals. Concentrating on her newest pack member, Katherine, she established a mental connection. In Constansa's opinion, Katherine was totally loco, but a huge improvement over their former team member Armand, whom Constansa felt had just tagged along for several centuries without ever being really useful. Theresa had questioned the wisdom in giving Katherine scout duty, but tradition demanded that the rookies got the worst assignments, and as Constansa had argued, considering how much Katherine hated anything having to do with Christianity, she would work twice as hard as any of them, itching to discover anything amiss. After all, Katherine had been the one most vehemently opposed to sequestering Elisabeth in a convent, and would look for any excuse to overturn that decision.

'Constansa here; what's your status, Katherine?'

'What the hell do you think my status is? I'm wet, cold and bored beyond belief,' Katherine complained. 'Next time, check the goddamn weather forecast before we go on an outing!'

'Situation is under control, I gather?'

'Basically yes. Security is tight and discrete. I've been watching them for a few days now, and besides being extremely keen on training outdoors in all kinds of weather, I haven't seen anything out of the ordinary. Discipline seems harsh though. I still think this idea sucks. She'll end up like some nut job if these fanatics get to mold her!'

'Just like the rest of us, you mean? You know better than anyone what kind of war we are fighting, and this place trains warriors – not couch potatoes. Better that she breaks here, instead of when facing her first demon once she's grown up.'

'You're the boss, but I'm telling you: this will come back to bite us in the ass…'

'Standard operating procedure,' Constansa mumbled to herself – but Katherine had a point. Considering Elisabeth's importance, it would be foolish to leave her here unguarded. Not opting for originality, Constansa asked Theresa for the securely chained, soundproofed box they had in the back. It was made of wrought iron, heavy, and just the right size for a Chihuahua – or in this case, a small gargoyle. She raised the divider between the driver and the passenger compartments and opened it very carefully – gargoyles hated being boxed up – but instead of being attacked by a ball of teeth and claws she just heard some pitiful sobbing from inside.

'I'm not talking to you' the gargoyle sulked. 'I thought you'd forgotten about me and that I would be in here forever!'

Constansa sighed to herself. The quality of gargoyles was going down.

'Listen carefully, you flying stone rat, if you don't want to be locked up and dropped on the bottom of the sea, where nobody will find you – ever – you better listen.' The gargoyle quivered, its tiny horns almost curling in submission. 'The girl in the back of the car is called Elisabeth. You are to protect her. If anything vaguely suspicious happens you are to contact me immediately and intervene as best you can. Because if you fail, we fail, and the bottom of the Atlantic is going to seem like a warm and cozy place for all of us.'

The gargoyle gulped. 'I'll do my best master, but am I supposed to do it alone? It could be dangerous, and look at me! I'd give a Chihuahua a fair fight!'

'Not to worry, I'll notice it when you die. So just make an effort. That way I don't have to reanimate you to punish you. And anyway, it's an old gothic style convent, so there's bound to be lots of other gargoyles for you to hang out with.'

The gargoyle didn't seem to appreciate the joke and looked more miserable than ever.

'Off you go, little rat, and make sure Elisabeth never sees you! She might take you for a demon and use you for target practice...'

Constansa was careful that Elisabeth didn't see the gargoyle as she snuck it out the front passenger door. She had no idea what approach the Grey Friars used when it came to revealing the harsh realities of the world to their charges. Breaking the news that the fairy tale world was actually the real one didn't always go down well with the youngsters. Small children adapted better than teenagers, so Elisabeth was lucky in having been discovered this young. Still, going away from her parents in the company of crazy strangers to parts unknown was bad enough for a 6 year old girl. Introducing her to gargoyles at the same time might be overdoing it slightly.

* * *

Two gorilla-sized gargoyles were looking down at Katherine as she was crawling through the bushes. Moving nothing but their eyes, their gazes met.

'Can I?' the younger one, named Eater-of-Nuns – Eon amongst friends – asked.

'Patience' the older one, Ravager-of-Babies – Rob – answered. 'This one's a scout.'

Seeing that Katherine was busy concentrating on a crystal, it pointed with a claw towards a small speck coming towards them. 'That one's the one we're looking for.'

Protector-of-Elisabeth – Poe – made no attempt at hiding as it flew towards the old building. The only thing Poe possibly hated more than being shut up in a dark, confining box was flying in the rain. It was sure that it would be struck by lightning on the way. Just its luck to have been made out of porous stone that didn't keep the water out at all. To its own amazement it made it safely to within a few flaps of the building. It was an old gothic church surrounded by several much more modern-looking buildings in the grounds around it, making the graveyard look a bit less spooky. Poe flapped around a little – safe in the knowledge that it would look just like a large bat to anyone on the ground – looking for a dry place to perch. After a little while it found a good spot – a nice and snug space between two of the largest and meanest gargoyles it had ever laid its eyes on. Their wings kept the rain out and their mere presence felt comforting. Relieved, Poe went in for landing – but it didn't even get its feet on the ledge before one of their tails shot out and wrapped the smaller gargoyle in a vicelike grip. Before Poe could as much as squeak, Rob turned its gaze upon it and Poe's crystalline eyes lost their light.

Eon hesitated. 'Quickly, you sod,' Rob hissed, 'before she notices it's dead!' Reluctantly, Eon turned his gaze on the lifeless statue and the light returned to its eyes. At the same time, Eon's former body crumbled into dust. Barterer-of-Bodies was everything but happy about its new form. This puny little shell was worthless compared to the last one it used. Grudgingly, it muttered that the prize they were aiming for better be worth it…

* * *

Below, the occupants of the limousine were spilling out on the parking lot outside the largest of the modern buildings. One of them – a tall dark haired woman in a military jacket – was kneeling down, holding her head, while the others were bristling with enough weapons to conquer a medium-sized country. Katherine was running towards them, weighted chains swirling in her hands, yelling something muffled out by the rain.

'What the hell was that?' Katherine's head was still ringing from the mental scream she had just heard. It had sounded desperately scared – and very close.

Constansa was bleeding from her nose as she used the car for support. 'Something bad.'

'As usual, then,' Katherine grinned. She had yet to see a mission go as planned since she joined this pack.

'I've asked a friend to watch over Elisabeth, since we have other pressing matters to attend to, and can't stick around forever. The plan was to drop the girl off, leave a guardian, and continue on our merry way,' Constansa explained. 'Except I think something happened to our friend. Hang on while I contact it.'

To her great relief she got almost instant contact with Poe. 'Status?'

'Everything's peachy,' the magical construct reported. 'Just had a pissing contest with the local gargoyles about perching places. I won.'

'Good, excellent noise level by the way. But in the future, save those battle cries for serious matters – or I might book that Trans-Atlantic cruise after all.'

'Sure thing boss, sorry about that, got a bit carried away. It's been a while since I saw some action!'

'Never mind, just stay focused. You're going to stay here a few years.' Was this that same sniveling creature she'd just had to pry forcefully out of its box? Never mind, the welcoming committee was approaching so she closed her eyes and concentrated for a few seconds to stop the bleeding, and had almost managed to wipe the blood away when they came to a halt in front of her.

Since the control Constansa had over the elements would keep her warm and snug in the middle of a snow storm, the sudden chill she felt in her bones couldn't be natural. Cullen was rummaging around with something inside the limo, most likely assembling the heavy machine gun that he'd liberated from the fuselage of a fighter plane. Knowing the kind of situations they used to end up in, Cullen had insisted on bringing it along – the gun, not the plane. Out in the yard, Katherine was sliding discreetly sideways, positioning herself to better strike the two rather burly priests in the back. Something was utterly wrong, but this place had been checked, double checked and triple checked by the most meticulous agents of the Church and came recommended, so who was she to judge? Her job was to deliver a package.

As tensions were rising, Constansa finished wiping off the blood and faced the abbess. She was surprised by her apparent young age. She seemed younger than Constansa herself – which would put her somewhere between 25-500 years of age – and was definitely not the ancient crone Constansa had expected. She didn't know what shocked her the most, the discrete makeup that was being smudged by the rain, or the genuinely friendly smile lighting up the young abbess's face.

The abbess didn't look like a nun at all, much less an abbess. Instead of the expected penguin outfit, she wore a female business power suit, with her long black hair in a tight bun. But she matched the picture in the file, and what she lacked in expected appearance she more than made up for in authority.

'The girl?'

'Her name is Elisabeth!' Constansa answered more harshly than she planned. Something was rubbing her the wrong way as she motioned Elisabeth forward. The abbess's smile froze as she saw the teddy bear Elisabeth was hugging tightly and snatched it from her.

'We will have no idolatry here,' she said curtly, and proceeded to rip the poor bear to pieces. Stuffing flew out onto the wet concrete.

Constansa's eyes narrowed, nostrils flaring – but Cullen placed his paw heavily on her shoulder, his presence keeping her from lounging at the abbess. In the corner of her eye she noticed Bartholomew moving up next to Katherine, to keep her from doing anything foolish as well.

'I am sorry, Mother Superior,' Elisabeth said in a thin voice. 'I don't know all the rules here yet, but I will do my best to follow them,' and, looking at her escort, 'It's just a toy bear. It doesn't matter.'

The abbess raised her eyebrows in astonishment while Constansa relaxed her grip on her sword.

'If I thought you would appreciate the hospitality I would invite you to spend the night, but I guess you would rather be on your way?' The abbess mentioned for Elisabeth to come with her, which she dutifully did.

Constansa spat on the concrete and nodded. 'We'll be off then, and you better take good care of her. I'll check up on how things are going – regularly.' It was neither the first nor the last promise that Constansa made and would not keep.

She knelt down in front of the child. 'Now, Elisabeth – be a good girl, and do what the Mother Superior tells you to do – and everything will be fine. You're a brave and smart girl and you can be proud of yourself. These nice people will take good care of you, and you will have plenty of friends among the other girls in no time.'

No reason for anyone to get more drenched than necessary, so one group clambered back into the limousine while the other headed for the main door.

The abbess could hardly conceal her glee as the limo disappeared from view. As the child watched, she grew taller and gaunter. The fingers resting on Elisabeth's shoulder curled and grew into long claws. Elisabeth gave a small yelp as they pierced skin and drew blood, but shut up when she felt the grip tightening.

'We will become such good friends, and nobody else in the whole world will know the secrets going on here. It will be such fun!' The abbess had bent down to look Elisabeth straight in the face and her forked tongue flicked in and out.

Elisabeth was glad the rain hid her tears.

VOLUME I: FROST MOON

Acolyte Tunang wasn't happy. Icy wind ruffled his parka as he sloshed through the mud towards the old hangar housing their HQ. The hunting trip he'd been looking forward to had lost most of its glamour. First, Sergeant Herlovsen had refused them permission to bring along their slave girls, and now he'd just found out that they weren't going to be issued any Battle Boosters either, on account of this being a 'low-threat'-mission. Fuck that, where was the fun in blowing shit up if you didn't have drugs and babes?

His foul mood wasn't improved by the ripe stench coming from the unclean slaves stacking metal crates just inside the hangar door. His firm grip on Lotte helped him calm down. Lotte was a fully automatic grenade launcher; the newest model from Kongsberg, accurate at ranges up to 2 km – not that accuracy really mattered with Tunang's preferred ammo. He paused, stroking her solid metal stock for a moment – and listened to it make a satisfying crunch as he used it to smash in the knee of the closest slave. The elderly male collapsed with a shriek. The heavy crate he'd been trying to push into place balanced precariously – the seconds stretching into an eternity – before falling down on top of the poor wretch. His outstretched arms broke like matchsticks, and the reverberating clang of metal against concrete mixed with the delicate sound of splintering wood. Tunang grinned, picturing the other unclean idiots having to clean up that mess, but tried to compose himself before entering the enclosed area they used for briefings. It wouldn't do if the brothers caught on to his not completely pious thoughts.

His attempts at composing himself were shattered by the large shape of Brother Bjerke approaching from the direction of the vehicle bay. Most of the Chosen were somewhat on the chubby side, but Bjerke was grossly fat. In his bright green, spotlessly clean mechanics uniform he looked like a large and ugly toad. It was never a good thing when Bjerke was happy. And right now he was grinning from ear to ear.

'Greetings Tunang, I hope you remembered to put on your thermal underwear,' the toad chirped. Tunang didn't follow.

Bjerke smirked smugly. 'Remember that slave you threw into the acid bath last week, because he smelled? Guess what – he was the only one who knew how the navigation systems worked. Which means that until we get a replacement specialist, the war-rig isn't going anywhere. So you're going out on the snowmobiles! With you on point. Since it's your fault.'

Tunang was fuming, but held his tongue. He knew that Bjerke was trying to provoke him into doing something stupid. Bjerke hated upstarts like him, who had clawed their way up from the orphanages. And while Bjerke couldn't dispute the purity of Tunang's Voice, he could do his best to make his life miserable. And what was the big deal anyway? It was just a slave. It was just like when he'd tossed his girlfriend's dog into the oven, when it didn't quit its damn yapping and his girlfriend went totally mental on him and he had to get physical. 'Note to self', he thought; 'remember to send her flowers and a new puppy – she ought to wake up from the coma soon.' You had to have standards, and if something wasn't up to standard, it had to be dealt with.

Snowmobiles? This was getting worse and worse. According to the weather forecast, a bad storm was coming up, and as trailblazer he'd have get off and on the damned machine the whole time. The problem was those new damned Italian combat armors they had been issued with. Strong enough to withstand 10mm shells and with a power field supposedly capable of stopping most energy weapons. The problem was that Italians knew nothing about how to make stuff work in sub-zero temperatures. The internal thermostat went haywire below zero and burned out the batteries in less than 5 minutes. Not really a problem as long as he'd be sitting plugged in to his snowmobile's power plant. Slightly more awkward when he'd be working unplugged, due to having to jump on and off the damned snowmobile all of the damned time. This was going to be a long and cold hunt. Pure joy, wading around in 20-30 kilos of Kevlar and useless electronics…

* * *

Sergeant Herlovsen was grinding his teeth as he watched his men fasten their supplies to the snowmobiles. He prayed that they wouldn't meet anything more dangerous than snow bunnies. And if those bunnies turned out to be hostile, he wouldn't put his money on his men. Men? More like spoiled brats than men. These were the Chosen, the kids not only blessed with Hearing and Speaking, but also coming from the families that ended up on top after the Chaos. Not all of them of course, just a handful of fat, lazy and spoiled kids looking forward to filling the rig up with slave girls, themselves up with combat drugs, and roar through the refugee camps, shooting at anything that moved. They deserved this mission. Only too bad he was the one who had to babysit them. Any causalities would have to be explained to the Grey Brethren. That was why he'd made Tunang point man. He was an orphan, so mummy and daddy wouldn't go all apeshit bananas if little Tunang died horribly. That and the fact that Tunang was a sadistic little prick who deserved some karma payback.

Herlovsen wasn't particularly superstitious. A lifetime in service of the Church had made a cynic out of him. He had realized that God most likely was a royal bastard that had stopped caring a long time ago, and since Herlovsen was too old be Awakened with Voice and Hearing, no one had caught on to his less than complete piousness. Still, he had noticed that it was rarely the nice soldiers who had their guns jam at the wrong moment. It could be because those were also the ones that usually maintained their gear properly, themselves, but the little things like that sort of added up. Herlovsen had a tiny glimmer of hope, deep inside, that he could buy himself a little goodwill in the eyes of Fate by helping her ever so slightly along.

Herlovsen counted heads and saw that they were all there. He blew sharply on an old sports referee whistle to get their attention.

'Attention, you maggots,' he roared, frowning. He wasn't too impressed with the amount of attention he was getting. 'Let's be honest about this. I hate babysitting you, just as much as you hate being babysat by me. I don't care what you think about, and I am not even going to report you if you hate my guts, as long as you follow orders and survive. If anything happens to you idiots, my ass is on the line. And when my ass is on the line, your asses are on the line. Understood?'

Motioning towards the snowmobiles he continued 'Since it is Tunang's fault that we're going on the snowmobiles, he will have the honor of riding point and blazing a trail for the rest of us!' Herlovsen was surprised by how cheered they looked by this. Did they really hate Tunang's guts so much that the thought of his misery overrode any concerns about the fact that they would be out in the storm as well?

'Raise your arms, those who've been out hunting before.' Most of them raised their arms.

'You!' Herlovsen pointed at Jespersen, one of the older boys. Tall and thin, with red-blond hair and huge outstanding ears. 'What was your last hunt like?'

'It was awesome, Sir! We had the rig loaded up with girls and just shot at anything that moved. First time I got to use combat boosters too! It is a bit hazy, but I think we had some helicopters above us finding targets for us. Not sure about that, Sir, sorry.' Jespersen got a dreamy look from reminiscing about good times.

'Good.' Herlovsen turned to Giske, another fresh-faced, Pure recruit. 'And you, what do you think will be different this time around?'

'Um, Sir, not much Sir. We will be outside in the storm on the snowmobiles Sir. And I guess we won't have any friends in the air, Sir' Giske looked a bit worried

'Correct, but you forgot the worst part. You forgot about The Silence.'

'What's The Silence?' the huge-eared kid asked nervously.

'Excellent question, Jespersen. Maybe some of you will survive, after all. I was starting to have my doubts.' Herlovsen made an artificial pause and put on his best schoolteacher expression. 'I'll take this from the beginning, so I can be sure that you follow me. Ever since the Awakening, the Lord Allmighty has Chosen some of the children of the Pure Families, blessing them with Sight, Voice and Hearing. And let's not forget the orphaned Chosen Ones, like Tunang – whose parents sacrificed themselves in service of the Church, the Lord rewarding them with the Choosing of their child.' Herlovsen knew this was utter bullshit; a useful lie fabricated to make sure the so-called Pure families remained in power, but he continued, unfazed. 'This is why you can hear and feel what your fellow Chosen think and feel. At the same time, the Lord chose to punish the Unclean, burdening them with Hearing but no Voice with which to speak.'

Herlovsen couldn't see the green blob that was Bjerke anywhere close, so he decided to cut down on the propaganda. 'You have been hearing the Voices of the other Chosen all of your life, probably even when you were in your mother's womb. As you've noticed, the strength of various people's Voice differ, and this strength is reduced by distance. Probably why no one wants to bunk with that loud-mouth Tunang, eh? Well, we are going out into what is called the Silent or Dead Zones. So named because they are so far away that the Voices of the Congregation can't be heard.

'This is why we have been give one of these!' In his hand he hold a small coin shaped yellowish crystal. 'This is a Booster. No, not a combat booster. Voice Booster! It boosts friendly Voices so that we will still be in touch with each other. Your own Voices are so weak that out there, without this little crystal, they wouldn't be much stronger than those of the Unclean!' This was heresy, so Herlovsen hoped Bjerke was terribly busy with something else. 'They are extremely expensive to make so we only get one, and naturally it is my responsibility to look after it.' He sighed, putting it into its assigned spot in the ridiculous looking helmet that was specially designed for it. Herlovsen felt like he might as well be wearing a huge 'Shoot me' sign.

'Sir, why are you telling us this, Sir,' Giske asked. 'Aren't we just going out on an ordinary hunting trip? Sir?'

'The reason is that the Infidels have been acting up recently and have become much more aggressive with their ambushes. And since most of your fathers sit on the Council of Elders, they've got ways to keep their sons from being thrown straight into the frying pan. They requested that their commander had to have experience from operations outside the Safe Zones. So you got me! And the assessment of my performance will not be affected by whether you hate me or not. Only on how many of you I manage to keep alive – and reasonably healthy. All else is secondary.'

Herlovsen walked slowly up and down the line of gathered boys, glaring at them with narrow eyes. Time to scare them into shape. 'Now – if we should get ambushed, or the shit hits the fan in some other way, our enemies are most likely bright enough to take the out the Booster – that is me – first. So, if my Voice suddenly disappears, listen for my physical voice – and get your asses back to the base any way you can. Whatever you do, do not start to listen to anything you might hear in the background. Because there are other Voices out there. Alien, demonic Voices – and you will be utterly lost if you start listening to them. And make damn sure you don't get captured! We found and rescued a missing patrol a while ago. And I guess they wished they hadn't surrendered. After capture, the Infidels had gouged out their eyes, put insect eggs in the cavities, and sewn the lids shut. It took a while before we could find and rescue them, so by the time we got there, the larvae had hatched and grown fat, feeding on their juicy brains. Not a nice way to go!' There was a reason why he bothered to go on about what to do if the Booster went down, meaning he was blown to bits. If a whole patrol disappeared, especially containing whelps of some pedigree, there was a remote chance that the Grey Brethren would actually bother to summon his soul for a report about what had happened. Herlovsen would rather minimize the chance of that happening, so if he could part with some advice that would let at least one of the kids make it back to report what had happened, he would.

'Our mission is simple enough,' he continued. 'The last known wolf pack between here and the Swedish border has been spotted by a scouting patrol. Why they couldn't just kill those wolves themselves somebody else will have to explain to you. We have been given coordinates to follow that should put us in the middle of their territory, and orders to destroy anything we encounter that's larger than a field mouse. We have a schedule to keep, but are permitted detours if we stumble across anything worth investigating or exterminating. This we will not do. We will slavishly follow the path described, blithely ignoring anything out of shooting range. Doing that, we – I – can blame whoever planned this mission when everything goes belly up. There is a possibility that the pack may be led by a werewolf. Each of you has therefore been issued with a single magazine of silver ammo. You know as well as I do that the ammo is useless, so just stow it somewhere. If one of those puppies turns out to be a super nasty puppy, just feed it a grenade. Even werewolves have trouble regenerating after being torn to shreds.' Satisfied with having their utter attention Herlovsen began stowing his own gear, including the crucifix they'd all be kissing before going out on the mission.

* * *

It didn't take long for Tunang to be soaked from top to bottom. Whether it was sweat or wet snow that caused it he had no idea, and his hands had gone numb a long time ago. At least they had reached the top of the hill and he was looking forward to blowing off some steam on the downward slope. 'Last man down scrubs the toilets,' he yelled before pushing the throttle.

As the scooters raced ahead, Herlovsen paused, looking down the narrow valley. There was a lull in the storm that gave him much better visibility. 'Perfect place for an amb....' he thought as two trees shook and Tunang was thrown of his snowmobile. The armored youngster did a double backflip and crashed into Hoseth behind him, the two of them tumbling off of their vehicles. The now riderless snowmobiles veered over the edge with a roar of spent gasoline, ending up as twisted hunks of screaming metal on the bottom of the valley.

'Nine,' said a person watching through binoculars from a safe distance. 'And that's before we start the fireworks.' He flipped a switch.

Suddenly the world exploded with small arms fire and Herlovsen felt several impacts dissipated by his armor. Several of the kids had even remembered their training and were trying to use their snowmobiles as cover from enemy fire. This was somewhat easier said than done, ambushed on a steep slope covered in deep snow. Herlovsen saw that Sørum had the presence of mind to think about a counter attack and was looking to lob a grenade towards one of the positions they were being attacked from. Sadly, he first lost his footing and then his grenade as he was trying to maintain balance. Herlovsen winced as the boy fell and landed on top of the grenade, just as it went off.

* * *

'Eight and counting' the watcher's buddy chuckled as he got the obvious officer in his rifle sights and pulled the trigger.

Herlovsen was knocked to the ground by a powerful blow and rolled down the hill, finally ending up next to the body of Tunang who was lying very still with his head at an awkward angle.

'You missed, Tor,' the watcher commented. 'He's still moving!'

'Damn it Geir, I wasn't trying to kill him! Only knock out the Booster. You know I don't kill in cold blood!'

'I wonder if the point man would agree with you about that,' Geir said.

Tor was too busy watching the hunting party doing eight different interpretations of Bambi On Ice to reply. They were in total panic, shooting wildly.

'Put down those binoculars,' Tor hissed. 'We'll see the next part perfectly well without them, and if these clowns have any training they'll be deploying defense drones any second now. Those drones are programmed to spot any kind of viewing devices and blow them to kingdom come!'

* * *

Herlovsen was trying to get his bearings and assess the situation. Surprised that he was still alive – and even more surprised about how indifferent he was about it – he carefully touched the top of his head to find out how bad the damage was. To his amazement the moisture sticking to his gloves was just melting snow, not blood and brains. It was just the top of his helmet that had been blown away. The part containing the Booster. The enemy knew what they were doing.

Looking around, trying to get an overview, Herlovsen realized this was no ordinary ambush. Except for the shot that took out the Booster, they were being fired upon by toy guns. And why didn't the ambushers rush out of their hiding places to finish the job? He saw that most of the kids had remembered his speech. They were scrambling up the hill, getting out of the line of fire, eager to get started on the long trek home. Dahl, an annoying little kiss-ass, was rummaging through his packs, signaling to Herlovsen that he had the retreat covered. He pulled out two large metal balls, which he started to fiddle with. Herlovsen winced, looked up, and got a sinking feeling as he saw how much snow there was on the slopes around them

'Dahl, cease that immediately,' Herlovsen bellowed. 'It's a trap! You'll kill us all!' But it was too late. The defense drones had been activated and their sensors immediately located the camera high up on the mountain side.

'Up', he yelled. 'Everyone! Out of the valley!' He kept roaring and waving franticly, but his words were drowned out; first by the shrieking sirens that went off from the vigilant drones, then by the thundering explosions going off as their mini missiles hammered the area around the camera, then lastly by the roaring avalanche that the explosions caused.

Most of the patrol noticed Herlovsen's frantic gesturing in time and got themselves to safety. Not so with Dahl. He was looking at Herlovsen, dumbfounded, trying to understand what he'd done wrong, when he was buried by a ton of merciless snow.

* * *

'Seven,' Tor said, a smile in the corner of his mouth as he packed down his rifle.

'Cool,' his brother said, raising an eyebrow. 'Now I get why you insisted on us going through all that hassle to get that camera up there. Fun way of doing this. But can I ask a really dumb question? Why are we bothering to make this ambush so complicated? Why didn't we just start the avalanche when they were at the bottom of the valley? Now most of them are getting away.'

Tor sighed, giving Geir a weary look. 'Come on, Geir. What do you think would happen if we wiped out an entire patrol? Somebody back at HQ would eventually start wondering about what had happened to them. Maybe they'd start sending out slightly more talented scouting parties? Hmm? How long would it take them to find the remains of the ambush, do you think? And do you think they wouldn't make sure to have a proper Cleansing of this whole district in that case? They might even start wondering how a cell of the Resistance can be active right under the nose of the local constable - which is you.' Tor poked Geir's chest. 'They might even manage to do some basic math and find out that this district is the last known location of the said constable's brother, who was dismissed in disgrace from the Special Forces. Do you really want that kind of attention, just for keeping old Ingjerd happy and saving a few wolf pelts?'

Geir shook his head.

Tor continued packing his gear, slinging the rifle bag over his shoulder. 'Now, the thing I'm counting on, is that these clowns have a somewhat intelligent commanding officer. He can blame the casualties on the avalanche, reckless driving and equipment malfunction, instead of admitting to running straight into an ambush. Remember, until recently I was one of those goons. I know how they think.'

* * *

Herlovsen took stock of the situation and gathered the boys around him. Here was a fuming Berg, a battered Hoseth, a terrified Jespersen, a less cocky Giske, as well as Bokalrud and Nielsen. Those six were all that remained of his patrol. Snowmobiles, tents and most of their weapons and gear lay buried under tons of ice and snow – and they were far out in the Silent Zone. Time to head home with their tails between their legs.

'Homewards, lads!' Herlovsen waved back towards the base.

'Sir, are we accepting defeat by primitive animals? Sir?' Berg gaped at Herlovsen.

The officer raised an eyebrow at the soldier with the wounded pride. 'We are not being defeated by wild animals, we are being defeated by common sense. Tunang drove carelessly and started an avalanche, while Sørum was a klutz and blew himself up. Not a whisper about us being shot.'

'Of course, Sir – but why?' Berg looked confused.

'Because the people attacking us knew exactly what they were doing,' Herlovsen explained slowly. 'If the shot that took out the Booster had been an inch lower, I would have been dead. They left the rest of us alive on purpose. Now, if we report back what really happened, there will be a Cleansing. And since we were the ones that made contact with the enemy, we will get the honor of being pathfinders. If we do that, my guess is that our ambushers will stop fooling around and play hardball with us. Now, do you really want to challenge the people who set up that ambush further?'

Berg shook his head.

'Good, didn't think so. So we all agree that Tunang caused an avalanche and Sørum blew himself up. Get walking, it'll take us long enough to get home as it is. As long as we keep moving, nobody should freeze to death, and if we have any luck somebody will notice that our booster is down and send out a rescue team.' Herlovsen gestured, and the seven armored figures begun their slow trek back home.

* * *

Further up, the wind was picking up again. Dry snow whipped around Tor's legs while he packed his gear. As he was about to strap on his skis, the terminal strapped to his arm starting blinking.

'What the fuck?' he said, staring at the multicolored dots on his screen in disbelief. 'Who the hell is out in this weather? Nobody with dull intentions, that's for sure,' he muttered to himself.

'Geir!' He threw a chunk of snow at his preoccupied brother. 'The sensors have spotted activity in sector 9! We check it out on the way home.'

* * *

In a bunker deep under The Town, the hologram of Cardinal Mikkelsen was calmly stroking his well-groomed beard as he scowled at a squirming General Løvholt, who looked more and more uncomfortable by the second. The guards almost felt sorry for him. Almost.

'Let me see if I have the facts straight.' The cardinal was using his most sugary voice. That never boded well. 'You, my dear General, let Elisabeth – the Prodigal Witch of our generation, trained to be a merciless killer by you personally – go off on a trip to the Silent Zone, only accompanied by two Warders? Ignoring my specific orders – to make sure that her Warders were homosexual males? Or are you claiming that you didn't read her file thoroughly, and just happened to miss that part? Hmm?'

'I don't have any gay soldiers,' the General whined. 'We purged them a long time ago!'

'Are you arguing with me, dear General?'

'No, Your Excellency, I beg forgiveness. But in my ignorance, I can't see what I could have done differently!'

'Let me continue. And do not interrupt me again!' Mikkelsen looked impatient. 'You gave her leave to equip herself with our most powerful sacred artifacts from the Vault. Then, when you lost contact with her Warders, you waited two days before reporting her missing? If I wasn't sure of your predisposition towards small boys, I would suspect you of being in cohorts with her.'

The general reddened. 'My apologies Your Holiness, but I thought I was following orders. You have imprinted upon us the importance of making our own decisions and not to bother you with trivialities. I was certain of reestablishing contact quickly!'

'The General has a point.' The third person by the throne-like holographic projector spoke. General Løvholt relaxed visibly as he got support from Sister Leine, Cardinal Mikkelsen's prophetess – and former mistress, which had lasted until her skin condition made her sickly stench unbearable. 'With all due respect, Your Excellency, you have repeatedly told us to handle things ourselves. There's not much harm done. Out where we lost her, there's only wilderness and the Troll Mountains. None of the artifacts she stole allows her to fly or teleport or anything like that, so she is out there somewhere. Alone. With few supplies. We will find her quickly, Your Excellency, especially since she has no wilderness training.'

'Thank you for your wise words sister. I have a hunting patrol out looking for her as we speak!' The General was clutching at straws, and the Cardinal broke out in mocking laughter.

'Those boys of yours are useless! Let us pray that they do not encounter anything hostile out there.'

'Does Your Excellency wish me to summon some hunter demons to fetch her?' Sister Leine asked eagerly. Though her cowled robes were of excellent quality, it was hard to believe that the creature hiding inside was human. The voice was croaking like a toad's, and her sweet, pungent stench reminded people of the sewers. Still, she was the Bride of Jesus for the Church of Norway – or what remained of it anyway – and very few people were keen on ending up on her bad side.

'No. Remember what happened in… Where was it? Larvik, or some such place? The last time you lost control of a pack.' Cardinal Mikkelsen sighed. 'Not a single being survived! Even the hamsters had been flayed alive. I want her back, preferably alive, and not inside the stomach of a random demon!'

Their musings were interrupted by a long drawn shriek of pain and the distant din of battle. The guards inside the throne room had assumed defensive positions around the door, but were waved away by the Cardinal.

'That, my friends, I believe is the answer to our problems. I have taken the liberty to invite the infamous Katherine to join us tonight,' Cardinal Mikkelsen said smugly. General Løvholt paled at the mention of her name.

'The Castrator?' Sister Leine gasped, getting an affirming nod from Mikkelsen, who raised his jeweled wine goblet to his lips, hiding his smile.

'Your Excellency, please enlighten us as to why you have let our greatest enemy inside the Bunker. She'll slay us on sight!' General Løvholt needed a table to steady himself on

'Hardly. You see, Katherine is a huntress. She hunts for the fun of it. And since she is quite good at what she does, she has a hard time finding prey dangerous enough to challenge her. That is why she has been making trouble for us. We, quite simply, are the most interesting prey in her vicinity. Now, I have faith that Katherine will find it more amusing to chase down a runaway Elisabeth than us,' Mikkelsen said calmly. 'If not we have a problem.'

The Cardinal chuckled, and his hologram mirrored him. As if he would put himself in harm's way! Løvholt had outgrown his use – except possibly as an example – and Leine was starting to scare him, truth be told. He had constant nightmares that she somehow broke the magical seals on his bedroom door and slithered into his bed. Ugh, just the thought made him shiver! He already had replacements lined up, in case Katherine should end up being pickier than expected in her choice of employer.

'Katherine is more than skilled enough to catch Elisabeth for us, and sending her on this errand will keep her out of our other operations for a while. Now think happy thoughts! About unicorns and rainbows and things. After all, Katherine's Hearing is exceptional, and you probably don't want her to catch onto what you're really thinking.' Another good reason to have this expensive holographic telepresence setup. It wouldn't do if Katherine found out what he really intended for Elisabeth…

The ornate double doors exploded inward. Through the smoking rubble came a menacing silhouette in battered, weird battle armor. Bloody chains swung from its left hand and its right fist was clenched, dripping red. It strode purposefully into the middle of the chamber. With a hiss, the helmet was withdrawn into the armor.

'Cardinal.' The wearer shook her head, unleashing a wave of blonde curls as she approached the trio. Leine and Løvholt were almost hiding behind the huge, beautifully carved chair containing the cardinal's hologram. 'You really need to get better guards.'

The armored woman walked straight up to the pale-faced military commander. 'General, give me your hand,' she ordered. It didn't even occur to him to refuse. She slapped what seemed like a pair of torn, bloody bags of skin into his outstretched hand, and Løvholt's paleness got a tinge of green to it.

'Your guard might want these back,' she said matter-of-factly. 'I am sorry about the mess. I am perfectly aware that my ass looks good in form-fitting battle armor, but I won't have whelps thinking dirty thoughts about it. He might survive to learn his lesson if he gets help quickly enough.'

Having emptied her hand, Katherine started poking at one of the smooth, red jewels embedded in the armor. The form-fitting, leather-matte carapace looked like something from a mad scientist-wizards dreams. Etched with runes and embedded with jewels and crystals, it looked more appropriate for a decadent costume party than a battlefield. She finally got the cabochon-cut little fortune loose and put it in Løvholt's other hand.

'And this,' she continued, 'is blood money for the family of the other guard. Tell them he was a brave young man who died quickly and painlessly, doing his duty, protecting his comrade from attack.' Katherine closed Løvholt's hand around the jewel. 'And, General? If I hear anything about you keeping it, I will personally shove it so far up your ass that you will spit it out again. Understood?'

Løvholt was shaking, but managed to nod.

Katherine turned towards Cardinal Mikkelsen, nodding as if she expected him to be represented by a hologram.

'You, Cardinal, I am almost impressed with. You know that I'll happily slay your two lackeys here, before your guards can even manage to see what happened. So I figure you've gambled on inviting me here for a reason. Perhaps you have more interesting prey than a penguin and a shiny-arse to divert my bloodlust?'

'Elisabeth.' Mikkelsen almost whispered.

Katherine exploded with laughter. 'Have you idiots managed to lose her?'

Mikkelsen nodded.

'All right. This might be fun enough. Obviously, you already know I have a past with her. It's been a long time since I had anything to do with her, though, and that is why you chose me, huh? Well, I messed up pretty badly regarding her, myself, so you'll get no snide comments from me about you folks fucking up.' She paused for a moment – then came to a conclusion. 'Ok. I'm in. Background info and payment in stem cells deposited at the usual place?'

'When you check you'll find the payment already deposited. I've prepared a dossier.' Mikkelsen motioned to a folder lying on a nearby desk. Katherine picked it up and started paging through it.

The Cardinal kept talking. 'Included is a list of artifacts stolen by Elisabeth. We would appreciate the return of all of the Church's property. There will of course be a bonus for that.'

'Need her alive or dead?'

'Preferably alive. Of course, we can try to bring her back to life if most of the body is intact, but resurrection is such a hassle. So, rather alive would be ideal.'

'Can do.' Katherine whistled as she saw the treasures Elisabeth had equipped herself with. The girl was packing. Maybe nothing all that useful in her current situation, but some of that gear would not be going back to a church vault anytime soon.

Katherine kept reading the files as she walked out through the smashed double doors, mumbling to herself that she would have to summon the pack for this one. She surprised herself by feeling the tiniest flicker of life from her conscience, for the first time in years. It seemed like Elisabeth had grown up to be the killer beauty Cassandra and the gang had expected her to become. They never kept their promise to check up on her, but who could have expected that the Awakening would erupt just a few months later? If Elisabeth was still alive, it ought to mean that she could take on a dragon and probably win – at least if it didn't cheat. This would be an interesting hunt.

Once Katherine's footsteps had died out, the silence in the bunker was deafening. Sister Leine finally broke it with a question. 'Maybe we should recall the hunting patrol?'

'Too late,' the General replied. 'They are already out in the Silent Zones. Luckily, those zones are huge and mostly empty. We can only pray that they will not encounter anything out there,' Løvholt shrugged.

As his lackeys left the chamber, Mikkelsen turned off the hologram and turned his attention to the creature reaching out too caress his cheek with its razor sharp claws – his newest mistress.

'Excellent, dear abbess,' he purred. 'You seem to have groomed her perfectly. It will be amusing to see if the rest of my predictions work out as planned. Then we'll have ourselves one very pleased master.'

'Elizabeth will do as expected' the abbess-creature hissed. 'The Council will be satisfied, knowing we did our outmost to retrieve her alive. Worst case scenario, she dies. Best case scenario, she opens the gate – and then dies. I made sure she found all the things she needed in the vault. All we need is patience and the Prodigy will be dead, the Huntress will be blamed, the Gate will be open – and we will be rewarded!"

* * *

In Sector 9, Elisabeth waded through the waist-deep snow. She promised herself – for the umpteenth time – that the next person who said anything about the "Great Harmony of Nature" would be flayed alive by her personally.

The worst of the storm was easing off, so she could see for more than a few yards. Hopefully, she had followed her navigation crystal well, and not lost her way again. Fair enough that the flower eternally embedded in amber, hanging in a necklace around her neck, kept her body temperature up and kept her from freezing to death. But her lovely dress was in tatters, and her amulet did not stop her nerve endings from signaling her brain that she was soaked and inappropriately clad for 20 degrees below zero.

Not that she had had much choice. In less than fifteen years she'd mastered a curriculum it took the other witches-in-training a quarter of a century to get the hang of. She might not have been in quite as much of a hurry if she knew what waited after graduation…

She was a War Witch. Tainted by nature, but allowed to redeem herself in the eyes of our Lord the Savior through infiltration behind enemy lines and doing the kind of jobs the Church itself was too squeamish to do, using their magical and martial skills – as well as their looks and their bodies – to fight the good fight! Or some such rubbish. Average life expectancy for a War Witch? Around two missions.

The Church believed in on-the-job training, so initially the War Witches were sent out on missions long before graduation. Who would expect that the helpless girl they had just rescued was a spy for the enemy? Of course, the Rebels caught on after a while, and their postings of the rape, torture and execution of underage War Witches was a propaganda disaster. The Church was forced to make changes, and introduced regulations that meant that until graduation, War Witch parents could veto any hazardous missions. If they were actually informed about the mission. The rich families always were, but even they were hesitant in showing anything less than total devotion to the Church.

Elisabeth, being an orphan, didn't merit such considerations. As a teen, she had served a long stint in a brothel the Church used as a cover for their clandestine operations near the court of Anglia, across the Poisoned Sea. For all she knew, the whole war might just be a charade to justify the depraved pleasures of the Pope and his Cardinals around the world. Pious lot these Cardinals, making war among themselves more often than not. Still, she'd done her duty, performing – and surviving – every harrowing task the Church set her to, through graduation and beyond.

Despite her many successes, she was not the most popular witch. Her reputation hadn't given her many friends among the witches, but at least the others kept their distance. And among the Cardinals, one should never underestimate the power of envy, nor the fear of change. Several of the more complacent members of the Council were worried that the Pope might be tempted to start a new crusade, now that he had a weapon as potent as Elisabeth under his control. They would much prefer to sit on their thrones, enjoying the blessings they had justly earned, instead of being called into some holy war. Thus, the Pope's best card had to be removed from the deck.

First they tried to send her somewhere in the middle of nowhere, where she could just be forgotten. When that didn't work, plan B was simply to send her on a hopeless suicide mission. Fortunately, she had caught wind of that plan, seen the bigger picture, and made sure to make herself scarce before her pruning could be implemented.

Elisabeth probably hadn't had to kill her Warders. Still, she consoled herself that they were better off reduced to ashes, far beyond reanimating, than being questioned by the Grey Friars about their failure. What the Friars would do to her, if she was caught, wasn't something she wanted to think about. She had been severely punished by them for running away in the past, whenever she had shown tardiness in returning home after a mission, and this time she had a feeling that her Prodigal status wouldn't save her life.

The biggest problem was that she knew her pursuers, knew their powers – and knew there were nowhere in the world where she could realistically expect not to be found. The only solution was to escape this world. And that was what she was trying to do, here in the swirling snow.

According to the ancient books she had read, there was a portal in a cave in the mountains nearby, which could only be opened when the winter solstice coincided with a full moon – like it would the following night. If she could only remove the wards put upon it by some ancient troll shaman, and calibrate it correctly, she could escape to the only place she could expect to be reasonably safe.

And that place was Hell.

As the snow storm eased off a little, Elisabeth noticed two moving shapes on the slope above her. Skiers. She sighed. She hadn't expected them to chase her down this quickly. She didn't have any time to waste – wading through the snow was slow going, and she would be hard pressed to make it to the portal in time, even without skirmishes like this. She glanced around, taking stock of her surroundings.

'Fuck me sideways' Geir said as he lowered his binoculars 'There's a teenage girl out there! And her Goth dress isn't exactly winter wear. It's a miracle she is still alive! What?' He glowered at Tor as his brother raised his eyebrows and shook his head.

'Of course we pick her up,' Geir continued. 'We got to get her inside and dry her up. When we are out here risking our necks to save those mutts and stumble across a helpless innocent girl we aren't leaving without helping!'

'Strange how those chivalrous instincts of yours only wake up when you have been without a woman for a while' Tor was obviously not convinced.

'Those knights were supposed to be chaste. And besides that. She's much too young for me. Has it become wrong wanting to just help someone?' Without waiting for an answer Geir pushed off towards the girl, but Tor reached out to stop him when he saw that she'd taken a small red jewel from a pouch and was holding it towards them.

'Hey! Wait! We're not hostile! We only wanted to see if you needed help,' the older brother yelled down to the Goth girl. Tor leaned in against his brother. 'That's a fucking War Witch,' he whispered. 'She'll melt this whole hill without effort. Be extremely careful,' he hissed through clenched teeth.

'Damn! So much for innocent and helpless,' Geir whispered back, cursing his luck.

Elisabeth smiled to herself. "Without effort" was a slight overstatement. The fire crystal she was holding would only focus her powers, so it would take some effort. But basically he was correct. Trouble was, she only had two of those crystals, and she didn't really want waste one of them unless it was absolutely necessary.

She lowered the crystal and Listened instead. They sounded ok. The older had a cold, military and somewhat rusty tone to his thoughts. Some normal parts of his Voice seemed to be missing, a strange phenomenon she had only heard before among long surviving slaves. Similar to her own Voice, in other words. No connection to the Church, no predatory intentions towards her. That he admired her corset was just an advantage. And he was quite handsome. The younger one had a very dull and subdued voice. Typical hillbilly, but his thoughts had a dependable sound to them. Both were without women.

This would be child's play.
She hadn't had time to study the ritual closely, but considering that it was in a grimoire bound with human skin, it was a fair assumption that some kind sacrifice would be necessary. These two randy rednecks could serve perfectly. And she needed some help with transportation – there was no way she'd make it to the portal in time, wading through the snow on her own. Note to self, remember to steal a broomstick next time.

'Well, hello there!' she smiled as opened the top button of her leather coat to put her amulet back around her neck, revealing more of her decidedly un-winterish décolletage. 'No offence intended, a girl can't be too careful, you know. And yes, very kind of you to offer some help! I could use a hand I admit.' She put on her best 'innocent whelp' face. 'The name is Elisabeth, renegade War Witch, by the way'

'My name is Geir, that's my brother Tor, and of course we will help a damsel in distress!' Geir was smiling from ear to ear, while Tor looked around thoughtfully.

'We'll need some kind of sledge,' Tor said, 'if we intend to get you indoors before you turn into an icicle.' A very pretty icicle, Geir thought to himself.

Said was done, and the brothers quickly cut of some branches and lashed them together into a poor semblance of a sledge. It was the best they could improvise on the spot, but there was no way it would hold together all the way home. They needed backup. The sledge would suffice to get them to a road, and then we would have to get someone to come and pick them. Elisabeth sat majestically in the sledge as Tor and Geir skied in front, dragging it through the snow. Both of them were glad Elisabeth was so light; they made good progress and it didn't take long before they came upon an old track, almost invisible in the sea of white.

Tor got the satellite phone out from his pack. Of course there wasn't any ordinary coverage out here, but the communication satellites that hadn't been shot down were still up there, and the military had their ways to hack and use them. A matched pair of sat phones and his sniper rifle were two of the parting gifts he had treated himself to when he was dismissed. They were pretty much invaluable for keeping in touch with home when they were out on patrol. With any luck, their youngest brother Bjørn, back at camp, wouldn't be so wasted on shrooms that he'd try to eat the phone instead of answering it…

* * *

Shrooms were unusually far down on the list of things that Bjørn cared about at the moment. He'd finally managed to bullshit Eirin into agreeing that sexual magic was the key to opening her up and tuning her into her wolfish side, and that her virginity was the main obstacle they had to overcome for her to finally be able to transform into the shape of her ancestors. For all he knew, it might even be true! He had no idea. The occult group – or "Heimdal Oasis," as the pretentious fools had insisted on calling it – which he'd been part of may have been a bunch of clowns, but they were good at staging things. He'd picked up a few tricks, at least, before making his tactical retreat from those loons.

The candles, incense and various trappings had done wonders – and Eirin's reluctance had finally caved in. Now she was just taking a quick detour to the toilet, and as soon as she was out of there, they'd begin the rite. Bjørn could hardly wait!

RIIIIIIIING!

'Fuck!' Bjørn swore loudly. This wasn't happening!

RIIIIIIIIING!

The damned sat phone! Which meant some kind of crisis…

RIIII...

Bjørn grabbed the handset and whined into it. 'Dude, you have no idea how much your timing sucks!'

'Never mind,' Tor said curtly. 'We need you to come immediately and pick us up with the truck.'

'Fuck that! If you want to fool around playing guerillas in this weather it's not my problem. I have more important things to do!' Bjørn rolled his eyes, itching to hang up before all his best-laid plans were for naught.

'We've a stumbled across a girl, freezing to death,' Tor said soberly. 'There's no way we can get her inside in time without the truck.'

'And how is that my problem?' Bjørn exclaimed as Eirin returned to the room. She looked questioningly at him.

He put his hand over the phone. 'It's my brothers. The idiots claim they need me to pick them up!' Fuck it – now that Eirin was standing next to him, he couldn't exactly explain what he was busy with. He put the phone to his ear again. 'And when did it become a good idea to pick up random strangers, huh? Strangers that can betray our hideout?'

'Shut the fuck up, Bjørn. Just get your ass moving and come get us.' Tor gave Bjørn the coordinates, and hung up.

'You should get going.' To Bjørn's surprise, Eirin didn't seem annoyed. 'They're out there for all our sakes!' Seeing his frown, she added 'There is no rush for me to be opened, Bjørn. And I know you'll have patience as well. After all, these things should not be rushed.'

* * *

The wind howled around the armored figures trudging through the snow – Herlovsen taking point, the rest like a row of ducklings after him. He'd made sure that his soldiers were roped together. Avalanches, reckless driving and carelessness with grenades? All of that could possibly be explained away. Losing one of the kids on the way home, however, couldn't. To make matters worse, the storm had picked up again. At least he'd had the good sense to bring along a backup battery. Not that it helped his poor, cold suit of Italian armor, but at least he could plug a nav computer in it and keep on course. Private Berg had volunteered the bright idea that they should just leave their armors behind, since they were next to useless in the cold. It was actually slightly tempting – but, considering what backwater they were stationed in, they would never get replacement armor. Besides, trekking back to base in nothing but their long johns didn't seem all that fun. At least the fancy hard suits kept most of the wind out. As long as they kept moving, they should be okay. Some frostbite would have to be expected, but cloning a replacement finger or a nose was a piece of cake.

Herlovsen felt a tug on the rope. He turned back towards Berg, who had stopped. Herlovsen cursed and waded through the snow towards Berg, getting ready to yell at him to get moving. 'What is the problem?' the sergeant barked.

'No idea, Sir!' Berg pointed behind him 'I stopped because Hoseth stopped.' Herlovsen cursed again, untied himself, and followed the chain back to its weakest link: Nielsen, who had collapsed in the snow. Nielsen was the youngest of the lot, barely old enough to have hair on his balls, a quiet and shy boy. At the moment he was lying in the snow, holding his head and moaning.

'What's your damned problem, Private Nielsen? Get back on your feet!' Herlovsen didn't have time for this. The angry impatience radiating from him could melt snow.

Nielsen writhed, whining desperately. 'The howls! Can't you hear them?'

'What the fuck are you talking about?' Something snapped inside Herlovsen. He took a deep breath, drew his sidearm and pointed the pistol at Nielsen. 'You get on your feet right now, private,' he said through clenched teeth. 'Every fucking one of us is going to freeze to death unless we keep moving. If you don't get up… Right. Fucking. Now. I'm going to blow your worthless brains all over the…'

'Um, Sir, hold on a bit, Sir!' Berg was trying to get Herlovsen's attention. A brave, well-intentioned, but not necessarily very bright move – seeing he now had Herlovsen's pistol aiming at him instead. 'I'm hearing something too, Sir! Some kind of weird howling – and it's coming closer!'

Berg's words probably saved Nielsen's life. Herlovsen took another deep breath, forcing his anger to cool, and looked around. Now that he paid attention, it seemed to Herlovsen that all his boys were hearing something. Sometimes, being Deaf was a bit of a hindrance. All of a sudden his motion detector went off. 6 large shapes were approaching them in the storm.

'Defensive routine Bravo!' Herlovsen screamed.

'Routine Bravo, my ass,' Berg thought. Bravo was something you used when you were defending a fixed position, with air and artillery support. Not while lost in the woods, with no visibility or backup! The howling was so loud he could hardly hear himself think. Great timing for their commanding officer to lose his marbles! Through the whipping blizzard, they could barely make out large shapes approaching. Berg heard some whimpering from his side – probably Jespersen – and the rifle shook in his hands as he opened fire.

'Cease fire!' An authoritative female Voice exploded in their heads.

Berg lowered his rifle – against his will – as a huge, four legged shape came lumbering towards him. Despite the filters in his helmet, he could smell the stench of blood and rotting meat from its pungent breath. For some reason, he began to think about a phrase in one of the books his sister had managed to hide away from the book burnings: 'eyes as big as saucers.' The author must have been trying to describe War Hounds like these. Massive monsters the size of draft horses. Mastiffs and Rottweilers, genetically modified to be many times their regular size, cybernetic abominations with strengthened skeletons and teeth. In constant pain, their bodies in no way evolved to support such size, and in theory controlled by chips implanted in their brains. Only an idiot would trust those chips, though, so their handlers used their Voices to command them instead. That had been that eerie howling they'd been hearing. The riders, communicating with their beasts. The Unclean didn't have War Hounds, which meant that these riders were on their side. Small comfort, since they'd just opened fire on them. Judging from the blood dripping into the snow, at least some of the shots had hit…

Berg was so focused on the Hound that he almost wet himself in surprise when its female rider jumped from her saddle, landed in front of him, ripped off his helmet, and put a knife to his throat.

'Are you the bastard that shot my doggie?' The rider couldn't be taller than 1.60, with short, completely white spiked hair, and ice blue eyes that were burning with fury.

'N-n-no, my gun is jammed! It was him,' Berg lied and pointed at Jespersen.

Quicker than the laws of physics should allow a beast of that size to move, the doggie pounced on Jespersen and bit off his upper half. Loud crunchy noises sounded through the storm as the beast chewed happily on it, armor and all.

'Erikka, control your damned mutt! These whelps are on our side,' the same authoritative female voice barked. It was Katherine.

'But boss, you said there was one too many of them! I was only being proactive.' Erikka pouted at Katherine as the pack leader rode towards Herlovsen.

'Sorry about that, sergeant.' Katherine halted her slobbering hound in front of Herlovsen. 'That was… Unprofessional. About as unprofessional as you lot starting to shoot before identifying your targets.' As she panned her gaze across the shivering soldier boys, she had trouble keeping her face straight. The Italian armor suits were obviously having trouble with their waste disposal systems, for the snow was turning yellow around more than one soldier's feet.

Herlovsen, however, wasn't scared. Actually, you didn't need any kind of special Hearing to notice how relieved he was. Finally, a superior officer! An officer that could take the blame for this disaster. Maybe there was a God after all…

Katherine turned her eyes on him. 'Sergeant, I can promise you that by the end of this mission, you'll fully believe in God – and curse his name,' she said with a venomous smile. 'Now tell me what you and your puppies ran into.'

Herlovsen made his report – not omitting anything, wisely enough – adding his reasoning as to why they retreated instead of pressing on. He had a gut feeling it wouldn't pay off if he tried to bullshit this beast-riding femme fatale…

His report made Katherine ponder. It could be a coincidence, but in her experience there were no coincidences. Somebody out there was wise enough to just turn the patrol around, instead of wiping it out. And that crafty she-devil Elisabeth on the loose in the area at the same time? Interesting combination. She was beginning to enjoy this mission more and more.

Still, there was no time to lose. Heaven only knew what Elisabeth was planning with the shinies she'd stolen. Among those baubles were basically all the things a novice portal opener could need, and with the winter solstice coming up tomorrow night, one didn't have to be a rocket scientist to figure things out. There was no way the direction Elisabeth was heading was random either. The only thing of interest in this direction would be the Troll Caves, supposedly named after the family of trolls that used to live there. Uninhabited for generations – and troll generations are long – with no one knowing what secrets they guarded. An educated guess would be that there was some kind of portal or rift in those caves, which Elisabeth planned to use to escape tomorrow night. Better catch her before then. And even if her theory was dead wrong, it would be easier to hunt Elisabeth down before she made it to the caves.

Katherine saw from the corner of her eye that Diane was going from hound to hound, soothing them and tending their bullet wounds. She was singing some kind of wordless song – extremely beautiful, a mixture of the howling of wolves and the singing of the arctic wind. It made the bullets fall out, one after the other, and the bleeding wounds closed before their eyes.

'Saddle up lads!' Katherine reached down to Herlovsen and swung him up behind her. The saddles they used on combat missions could seat two – if somewhat uncomfortably. No one would be left behind in case of a fallen hound.

'You're going to show us where the ambush happened.'

Herlovsen sat behind Katherine, Berg got Erikka, Hoseth shared hound with Diane, while Giske sat behind a huge blond guy, Harald. He had led the pack until Katherine defeated him in single combat, and still looked like the poster boy version of a Viking. Bokalrud rode with Monkey, a huge Serb with dreadlocks and enough bling to make a pimp envious. Nielsen had chosen the one that seemed most harmless, a misshapen dwarf called Ludvig, who had the head of an adult but the body the size of a toddler. Scary as hell, true, but less lethal looking than the others.

Soon, the six beast riders were dashing through the snow on the backs of their six slobbering hounds, six shivering soldiers holding on for dear life.

* * *

Bjørn squinted through the windshield. The rig he was driving was an old snowplow. Well, it used to be. Now it was converted into a vehicle of war that Mad Max would have been proud of. He was getting close to where he'd be picking his brothers up, and it wouldn't do if he ran them over instead of home.

Bjørn had a real bad feeling about this. For the zillionth time, he checked that his weapons were within easy reach, Desert Eagle? Check. Silver bullets? Check. Shotgun? Check. Cold iron shrapnel? Check. SquirtMaster 2000 with its neon pink reservoir filled to the brim with Holy Water? Check and fucking check!

It could not be a bloody coincidence that a damsel in distress should show up around now. Not with Ingjerd's prophecies about rains of fire and portals to Hell! Back in the days, Ingjerd was winning the lottery often enough that only a fool would ignore her warnings. Especially with a full moon coinciding with the winter solstice, and the ancient Troll Caves nearby. His family had been guarding those damned caves since forever. Only Tor and Ingjerd knew why, but at least these days they had sensors and remote alarms. No need to sit in a dull cave, waiting for nothing, freezing your ass off.

And this girl... No one travelled alone without being able to defend themselves anymore. It was just too dangerous. Typical timing, this happening just when they were making some progress, training the local kids. You never knew when the Church would start their missionary work again, sending out freshly anointed teams of Sirens and Rat Catchers to bring more children into its abusive fold. That's why they needed to train the kids – so they would resist all those seductive voices in the night. A few more months and the youngsters would have been safe, ready to just disperse into the woods and live off of nature when danger would rear its ugly head, conducting guerrilla warfare if necessary. Now, though – if things went south... Bjørn didn't want to think about it.

* * *

Herlovsen pointed. He was explaining where the shots had come from and where the sensors that had triggered the avalanche had been placed. Katherine barked out some orders, and her pack spread out to implement them. Erikka secured the copse of trees where the shots had originated, and saw that the automated weapon turrets had run out of ammo. Monkey sniffed his way to where the brothers had been watching the spectacle, and found both the casing of Tor's single shot and some of Geir's cigarette butts. The casing implied a powerful military weapon, while the turret guns were nothing but modified civilian hunting gear. It didn't look like an organized ambush by one of the many groups that hated the Church – more like die-hard mountain men that hated outsiders on principle. Most likely. And since half the night had passed, most likely was good enough.

It looked like the ambushers had left on skis. That meant it would be a piece of cake to catch up with them. Katherine felt no need to rush it. She'd rather let them get back to their den, where they'd think themselves safe and let their guard down. It was a common first mistake.

Katherine signaled that they should get going again. The hounds bounded almost playfully over the snow at great speed, and if Herlovsen and his men hadn't been strapped on, they would've had no chance of hanging on. As it was, the rookie riders were mercilessly tossed back and forth.

Nielsen had it worst. Ludvig was so small he didn't care about low hanging branches as they were crashing through the forest. Nielsen, however, stuck up above the saddle, and got all the branches and snow in his face. Earlier, he had removed the visor of his armor as the Italian garbage misted up and made it impossible to see anything. Now, he bitterly regretted that decision, and straightened himself up to put it back up – at the wrongest possible time. A large branch hit him squarely in the chest. If he hadn't been strapped tight, he would have broken a few ribs and been sent flying. Unfortunately for Nielsen, his lower body was strapped tight to that massive hunk of muscle and cyberware thundering through the forest beneath him. The soldier's spine broke with a dry, brittle crack, his torso flapping back and forth like a ragdoll, gurgling blood. Ludvig looked behind him, undid the straps, and simply let the dead weight fall off. The dwarf could have gotten good money for that corpse, but it would be impractical to lug it around for the rest of the mission.

The storm was threatening to obliterate the tracks, so Katherine told Diane to change. Diane removed her battle armor, looked up at the moon and started howling. Her already sharp features elongated into a long snout with nasty pointy teeth, and the rest of her grew – ending up as two and a half meters of fur and sharp claws. She dropped down on all four, looking like she could give one of the War Hounds a fair fight. In this shape she could track a fish down a river. With a whoosh she was off, following the scent – a silvery blur among the trees.

As the rest of them followed, Herlovsen was wracking his brain, trying to find a way to survive this madness.

'Who the hell are you,' he asked Katherine.

'Better question would be what the hell we are, and if I answered that, I would have to kill you. The less you know the better off you are. You know there's no way around that debrief by the Grey Friars for you, so you might want to start taking notes. The more unimportant details you can give, the faster you'll have your head off the block. And forget those thoughts about a hand grenade. They'll just summon your soul back from the dead. Then they will be really annoyed, and you don't want that.'

* * *

Bjørn drove as if the dead were breathing down his neck. The girl had confirmed his worst fears. No way was a city chick like her out here without a purpose. And how the hell had she survived out in the cold in those clothes? She should have been dead a long time ago. The rig was bouncing around like a rodeo horse – mostly due to his reckless driving. Having Elisabeth sitting next to him in the front seat, with all his weapons in her lap, didn't exactly calm him down. Not that he thought those weapons would do him any good…

Elisabeth looked at the SquirtMaster and nodded approvingly when he confirmed that it contained holy slush. After all, it wasn't that warm inside the rig either. The argument about who should sit up front had ended up with no winner, so Elisabeth ended up there with Bjørn while Tor and Geir were crammed in tightly in the passenger/storage compartment – neither of them happy about sharing the confined space with each other instead of a lovely – and significantly smaller – Elisabeth. Tor had already phoned home and briefed Eirin on the situation, and while she had no formal medical training, at least she could prepare blankets and some hot beverage. If you had any aspiration of training a troop of mountain guerrillas, some basic survival skills were necessary – like how to treat hypothermia.

'Home' was a former luxury ski resort cabin complex, rebuilt into quite the fortress. Lying atop a small hill with excellent view of the surrounding area, all ascents were carpeted with landmines and other traps. The former owner had apparently been rather paranoid. The place had extensive alarms, formerly connected to some long defunct security company. Tor had rewired it all into a pretty decent surveillance system.

Though the area wasn't completely lawless in theory, it was pretty close. There was the nominal presence of the local constables, Geir numbering among them. But they had no formal law enforcement powers any more. Their duty was to keep watch for any rebel activity, and file reports on any non-believers they discovered. Geir had done this dutifully for several years, until he got pneumonia one winter and missed a couple of reports. He was out of his mind with worry that the Church's wrath would come down upon them, and that they'd starve or be shot or worse – but, to his great surprise, nobody noticed. Their supplies came as scheduled. That's when Geir realized it was all a scam. The Church had enough trouble trying to keep their central areas secure to give a rat's ass about what happened out in the boondocks. Anything short of a full scale invasion would be ignored. Which meant that might made right out here. Or rather, if you had access to firearms and explosives, bright made right.

After Tor had been thrown out of the Special Forces in disgrace – he refused to talk about what had happened – he still had the war in his eyes. All he ever said about it was that he'd been to Hell and back. His brothers secretly wondered if he'd left crucial parts of him behind; there was hardly anything left of the bright, adventurous lad that had wanted some excitement. But his military experience was invaluable. He went into fortification mode as soon as he got home, and he didn't have to ask Geir twice to join him in taking over one of the big luxury cabins abandoned by their owners.

Tor busied himself those first few months, cleaning weapons and rewiring the old, useless alarms into triggering a variety of mines and booby traps. Windows were boarded up and tunnels dug between the different buildings, in case they'd get into a sticky situation. In the turmoil of the Cleansings, food and fuel were more valuable than weapons. That made it easy for them to scrounge up quite an arsenal of civilian hunting weapons left behind in the cabins, as well as some old surplus military equipment. Once his defenses were complete, Tor felt fairly sure that they'd be able to fend off anything short of a combined air and armor attack. He supplemented the excellent view they had of the surrounding area with a network of sensors for dark and stormy weather, and had even bowed down to Ingjerd's demands that the caves should be secured as well.

Though Geir – and Bjørn, especially – made plenty of snide comments about Tor's paranoia, they were secretly happy about it. They knew that thanks to him, they were as safe as one could be in these dangerous times. After the cataclysm, when the barriers keeping the many worlds of the cosmos apart had been torn down, there were more than enough things that went bump in the night.

There were always reasons for mourning, when people did the headcount every spring, to see which of their neighbors had survived the long nights. And they were fast approaching those longest nights. One didn't have to be very superstitious to think that something could be up when the winter solstice coincided with a full moon – the Frost Moon, as it was known.

* * *

Safe. Well, that would be if Eirin had remembered to turn off the booby traps. Bjørn stopped just outside the minefield and radioed her to make sure.

'Bjørn here, have you turned off the minefields?'

'Only one way to find out, honey,' a female voice replied.

'Yeah, fuck you too. Just make sure that you turn them back on immediately after we are through! I have a really bad feeling about this,' Bjørn mumbled.

Elisabeth cursed silently. Just her luck that the third brother already had some kind of girlfriend, and that she was around. Always more difficult to control two lovebirds if they were together. But what the heck, this was supposed to be her field of expertise. She just had to give it her best shot. Anyway, she was getting curious about these people. Folks that brought holy water on taxi missions, and lugged military sniper rifles around, weren't nobodies.

The massive vehicle roared up the hill and pulled to a halt in the yard between the picturesque timber cabins. They were almost buried in snow and looked like they came straight from a Christmas carol. A Christmas carol with machine gun nests – unmanned, Elisabeth noted – and barbed wire. The dark guest cabins were huddled in a semicircle in front of the brightly lit main building, and Elisabeth's attention was captured by the beautiful girl bathed in the light streaming from its open front door. With the light coming from behind her and her long red hair blowing freely in the strong wind, it almost looked like she had a halo. As Tor and Geir were cursing about soreness and stretching their legs, the girl motioned for them to hurry up with one arm, while the other was hidden behind the door she struggled to keep open in the storm. Probably with a weapon in it, Elisabeth thought.

'Hurry up! I don't want to let the cold in,' Eirin shouted and waved them in. When Elisabeth passed her, she gave the Goth princess a thorough, almost hostile look. Bjørn thought he could see sparks flying between the girls already. Catfight coming up! Eirin wasn't going to give up her position as "hottest babe around" voluntarily. And Elisabeth was a clear challenger for that title. Fair enough, maybe now his brothers would get off his back for flirting with the girls they had in. Normally there would be 25-30 people living here, mostly the boys and girls of the district receiving what passed for schooling these days. No more algebra or literary analysis; the curriculum was subjects like arctic survival and how to banish a demon. Most of the kids had gone home to their families to

celebrate the winter solstice - or "Jul" as some old timers insisted on calling it –
and only Eirin had stayed, on his personal request.

* * *

The three brothers – Tor, Geir and Bjørn – were the latest generation of the
Myrvang family, the family that had been the soul of the community for as
long as anyone could remember. There had always been a Myrvang as the local
constable, the priest was always a Myrvang, and among the youth the same
applied to the role as captain of the local soccer team. So when the world had
gone to hell, it was only natural that the community turned to the Myrvangs for
guidance. The only Myrvangs left back home at the time of the Troubles were
Geir and old Ingjerd, the brothers' great-aunt, who lived in her own cabin far
out in the forest. Tor had left home just before the beginning of the Troubles, to
volunteer for the militias, and saw action in all the places they could see go to
hell live on television. Bjørn, after his infamous proclamation about Myrvang
– which also was the name of the village – being nothing but a speck of shit on
the map, had left long before. As soon as he was old enough, he'd headed out
to seek his fortune in Oslo. Of all the lessons he learned away from home, the
most important one was discovering that the last place you want to be when
civilization breaks down is trapped in a major city. Beaten and broken, both
errant brothers had eventually returned to their ancestral community and the ski
slopes above.

Life out here was good, if not exactly safe. Luckily, the declining numbers of
ravaging bandits had made the district calmer over the last couple of years.
Banditry might have been a viable survival strategy at the start of the Troubles,
with easy pickings all around, but now, any settlements still standing knew how
to take care of themselves. You'd need military hardware to take them on, and if
you had that kind of hardware there were much richer pickings further south,
where there were still proper cities and crazy warlords paying people to fight
over them. So unless they did something to draw the omniscient gaze of the
Church down on them, they ought to be safe. Messing around with a few patrols
was one thing, but harboring a wanted refugee was something completely
different. That was just the kind of shit that would turn their tiny mountain
paradise into a charnel house. The Church was good at maintaining its fiery
traditions, and now they were backed up by modern technology that would've
made the original inquisitors squeal with delight. And like in Torquemada's
days, having a few bible-thumpers knock on your door was not a healthy
experience…

* * *

Once the others were inside, Eirin waited while Bjørn drove the rig into the
garage. The vehicle had no trouble weathering the cold, but he'd prefer not to

come back in the morning and find that a gaggle of metal eaters had made a feast of it. When he returned, Eirin closed the door behind them and discreetly returned the shotgun to the cabinet. She locked the door, bolted and barred it, before spitting on her index and drawing some sigils in the air, as they were stomping off the snow. The brothers looked like snowmen and Elisabeth resembled a drowned black cat.

'You must want some hot water and the opportunity to freshen up a bit, princess,' Eirin told Elisabeth condescendingly, raising her eyebrows at the newcomer's fancy clothes and jewelry. 'Just follow me,' she continued. 'I hope the accommodations will prove acceptable, your highness! The place was built by people who spared no luxury, at least.' Eirin lead the way to a huge, marble-tiled bathroom, with a Jacuzzi and everything. 'Yeah, the plumbing still works! Just throw your wet clothes outside the bathroom door, we'll dry them in front of the fireplace. There ought to be plenty of bathrobes in there.'

Ok, this was way better than Elisabeth could've hoped for. She decided to try, if possible, to spare these people. Maybe they had rabbits in cages, or a henhouse, or something. Blood was blood, after all.

Elisabeth started to fill the tub, and got herself out of her wet gown. She made a note to self that black velvet and lace – while perfectly viable in most situations – wasn't perfect for rough weather. Before allowing herself the luxury of entering the now steaming tub, she checked her shoulder bag. The book was still there, alongside the handful of amulets and jewels she'd grabbed. She could've aimed better. She had amulets that would protect her against lizards, and jewels that could cure poison, but nothing that could protect against bullets or turn her invisible or anything actually useful. She did have the fire crystals, though, and a few other combat crystals – and thanks to her navigation amulet, she wasn't hopelessly lost. She'd also brought along the grimoire that described the procedures for opening portals, as well as the candles and other paraphernalia she was going to need.

* * *

'So, lads - what's the plan?' Eirin was looking skeptically at them. They were lounging around the huge fireplace that dominated the combined living room/kitchen. They had covered the panorama windows with metal sheets, and hung them with video screens linked to the surveillance system.

'We couldn't really leave her out there to freeze to death, now could we?' Geir said, somewhat sheepishly.

'You damn well could have,' Eirin snapped. 'We've had this discussion before! We can't save the whole bloody world, but as long as we're careful, at least we can save our own goddamned necks!'

'Calm down, Eirin,' Tor barked, then continued in conciliatory tones. 'I know you aren't planning to murder her in cold blood. So what do you think is best?'

'Just throw her back out, of course!' Eirin's eyes flared.

Tor sighed. 'You might as well put a bullet in her head instead, then. That's kinder and quicker.'

'Eirin does have a point' Bjørn interjected. Kissing up usually paid off. 'We have a 5 star setup right now. We're so far out in the middle of nowhere that nobody can be arsed to care about us. Mostly because nobody who might care knows about us! We grow a surplus of food, we have clean water, our own hydro-electric generator, and enough firepower to chase away anything that goes bump in the night. But now, now we have a renegade War Witch as a houseguest. Tor, you know that the church doesn't allow it's servants to go AWOL, and you don't have to be the last of the Mohicans to track her here. So I'm thinking this is pretty much it for our anonymity!'

Bjørn cast a glance at Eirin. She was listening. 'Question 1: Can we trust her? I don't think she's going to slit our throats while we sleep. The question is more whether she'll keep her mouth shut about us. It really wouldn't help us if she goes around blabbing about those nice and friendly people near the Troll Caves that helped her out. We aren't that difficult to find if you know we're here.'

Was that a smile? Bjørn continued, feeling he was on a roll. 'Question 2: What the fuck is she doing out here? For all we know, unlikely as it is, she might be on a church mission. If she's from around Oslo, it doesn't make sense at all for her to be travelling in this direction. She should've been heading in the opposite direction, where there are more people and settlements, and much easier to hide. What is there to interest a War Witch out here, regardless of whether this is official church business or her personal pet project? Especially considering Ingjerd's prophecies about everything going to hell! War Witches are pretty much the top of the food chain; everyone is basically just running around and kissing their feet. For one to go renegade is unheard of! They aren't exactly very popular and need the protection the Church gives them, even though they can handle themselves well in a scuffle. So I think it is safe to assume that our helpless little waif here has some ulterior motives with her field trip. And I am willing to bet my ponytail that it has something to do with the Troll Caves – and that the timing isn't random either.'

Bjørn had all their attention now. It felt good to be taken seriously for once. 'Next question: Do we care? Most likely yes. Ingjerd tends to be accurate, and with a Frost Moon coming up it is likely that Elisabeth at least thinks that something special is coming up. So, how do we find out? Simple: We ask her.'

'But how will we know if she's telling the truth? If she is up to no good, she won't be stupid enough to tell us,' Tor said, frowning.

'Bingo!' Eirin jabbed a finger into the air, nodding approvingly at Tor 'Seems like some parts of your brain still receives blood.'

Bjørn gave her a sly look. 'Well, if you don't suddenly get access to your fabled wolf instincts, we'll just have to make her trust us. Which is going to be difficult – I know I wouldn't have trusted us one bit if I was in her place…'

* * *

The object of the discussion was soaking in the Jacuzzi, enjoying the feeling of warmth slowly returning. The bath felt divine; that feeling of ice melting, body-cell by body-cell – indescribable. Note to self, filed under "Future Punishments": Cold – a quite unique and horrible form of pain.

Elisabeth took stock of the situation. It could have been a lot worse. On the upside: She had found a group of heavily armed but friendly hillbillies that knew the area and had access to transportation. The downside was that she was quickly making herself dependent on the hillbillies. She was more of a prisoner than a guest, since there was no way she could get away from these people in this weather. And even if she did, she would have no chance of making it to the caves in time – not to mention that she needed sacrificial victims too. The plan was quite simple: Manipulate them into providing an armed escort to the caves, then sacrifice them to open the portal. What could possibly go wrong with such a simple plan? She tried to decide how to implement it. Said hillbillies would probably not bounce up and down with joy when she told them where she wanted to go. No, she would have to serve them some sob-story and win them over with her damsel-in-distress act. It had been working pretty well so far…

Elisabeth got up from the Jacuzzi. No need to give Eirin time to turn the men against her! She put on a fluffy bathrobe, large enough to drown in. Looking in the bathroom mirror made her frown. She looked like a Goth who'd spent a week-long music festival sleeping in a tent. Not good, in other words. She gave herself a thorough look, then waved her fingers and muttered some words in an obscure language. All of a sudden, her old makeup disappeared and a fresh layer was laid in its stead, accentuating her manga-girl look. Humming to herself as she was drying her hair, she mentally prepared the love spells she'd need to twirl those mountain men around her little finger. Elisabeth didn't really have any experience in how her glamour and love spells worked on females, but the principle should be the same. Live and learn!

Satisfied, she left the bathroom and joined the others by the fireplace. As they turned towards her, Elisabeth had to struggle to keep from laughing at their stunned faces. She felt like a wolf, casually sauntering in between an oblivious flock of sheep.

'Nice setup' Elisabeth said, nodding towards the video screens, trying to break the ice. 'I hope the surveillance's external only – don't want to have to worry about you boys peeping on us in bed or in the bathrooms!'

The brothers started babbling all at once, reassuring her that they were just external, and Eirin pointed out that she'd threatened to sneak around at night with a pair of scissors, mutilation in mind, if she caught anyone trying to set up a camera in one of the bathrooms. Somewhat embarrassed, Bjørn mentioned that this was a huge hole in their security. If anyone got through the perimeter, they had no way of tracking them inside the buildings. Eirin sneered at that and said that if anyone got inside they were fucked anyway, surveillance or no surveillance. Elisabeth refrained from commenting on that and sat down next to the fireplace, noting that Geir's gaze didn't leave her bare thighs for a second.

Elisabeth smiled at them. 'From the looks on your faces, I'm guessing that you're more than a little curious about what Dorothy is doing out here. Cause this sure ain't Kansas, and I don't see any dogs called Toto around either.' Seeing their confused frowns, Elisabeth continued 'Not big on Oz references? All right, I'll make it short and sweet, then. As you may have understood, I am – or was – a War Witch in training, but I discovered something horrible, and decided to run away. You see, the Church worships not only Jesus Christ our Savior, and the Heavenly Host – but also,' she whispered now, for dramatic effect, 'the powers of Hell!'

All Elisabeth got was a few raised eyebrows. She carried on, as earnestly as she could. 'Not a surprise to you, maybe, but quite a shock for me! I'm trained to be inquisitive, so of course I tried to find out more. I discovered that there's a real portal to Hell, right here in the vicinity, and that it will open tomorrow night! Those fools plan to let it happen, hoping to make a deal with the demons pouring out of it or take control over them or something equally insane. When did the Power of Christ compel anyone, without a few swords or gun barrels to back it up, huh? The idiots will fail, and it will be the end of every soul out here, hell maybe even on Earth – which is an acceptable danger for the Church, since it would be preferable to letting the heathens and infidels win. I won't stand idly by and let that happen, so I'm going to seal that portal before it opens – but I'm running out of time!'

You could have heard a pin drop to the floor in the following silence. The brothers had swallowed every single word, but Eirin wore a skeptical frown. The redhead noticed, almost smelled, that something was wrong. She felt a strong, almost nauseatingly musky smell coming from Elisabeth, a smell that obviously had a different effect on the menfolk than on her, judging from the way they were gaping slack jawed at the witch.

'So you are some kind of heroine, forsaking a life of luxury and power to save the world,' Eirin sneered. 'Pardon me for not buying that story.'

'I think it's a plausible story,' Geir said slowly – his gaze still locked to Elisabeth shapely thighs.

'The Church has a tendency to start playing with fire when desperate,' Tor chimed in. 'Considering the kind of people they've allied with in the past, this could very well be true.'

Elisabeth put on her most convincing face. 'And do you think I would be out here all alone, without an escort, if I was on a mission for the Church?'

'Just got a message from our friends in Oslo' Bjørn interrupted. He had been fiddling with the communication center while the others had been talking. 'Same crowd that tipped us about the patrol are saying that some supposedly dangerous terrorist, matching your description, Elisabeth, is on the run in this area. You've got quite a bounty on your head, so that part of your story is confirmed at least! Problem is, this place will be swarming with bounty hunters in no time.' He shrugged apologetically towards Eirin. 'So, assuming that the part about the portal is true as well, what's your plan? I am inclined to believe what you are telling us,' Bjørn said, with Eirin growling in the background, 'but if we're going to consider helping you, I just want a plan, you know – I mean, what are we going to do when at Ground Zero of a portal opening to Hell? Hopefully you've got something more solid than having us stand in a circle, chanting Ohm.'

'Well, I kind of do,' Elisabeth replied. 'You see, according to my research, back in the day, before us Homo Sapiens were the dominant ape on the planet, some kind of Troll shaman sealed off this portal. Now, those seals are so old that they're coming apart. If I can manage to reinforce them, though, we should be good for a couple of thousand years more!'

'Sounds way too easy,' Eirin objected. 'If anyone plans to let that portal open, all they have to do is send a regiment of soldiers to stop anyone from interfering!'

'But they won't be doing that,' Elisabeth explained. 'First thing you got to know is that the Church is one big charade. While the Pope and all the cardinals all serve some duke of Hell or another, they have to be discrete about it. Anyone caught red handed dealing with devilry are publicly condemned and punished. They think they need to maintain appearances – for the people's sake.'

'Yeah, but what they don't realize', Geir added with a grim chuckle, 'is that they're so hated anyway that people couldn't care less if they served Satan himself.'

'Exactly! So knowledge about a gate to Hell that is about open will have to be handled delicately,' Elisabeth continued intently. 'There isn't a Cardinal out there that could get away with s sending ordinary troops to something like that. It would have to be either a squad of Grey Brethren or their personal bodyguards. That means the number of enemies we'll face is going to be limited, but they may well be elite commandoes.'

'That's where we come in,' Geir said enthusiastically. 'We know the land like the back of our hands! No matter how well-trained and equipped they'll be, we'll have the advantage!'

'And what the fuck happens when the smoke dies down and we've won our little war, huh? How the hell are we going to keep the Church from wiping us out in retaliation?' Eirin was getting worked up again.

'Damned if we do, damned if we don't.' Tor said calmly. He had been quiet as tempers began to rise. 'Inquisitors of Christ or the Legions of Hell? The Church we know how to fight, at least. But,' he said and stood up, 'the middle of the night is no time to make decisions like these. Let's sleep on it and make a good decision tomorrow. In daylight.'

No one argued against such wisdom – they were all exhausted.

* * *

Elisabeth whistled under her breath as she looked around the guest bedroom. She room she'd been given was of the same luxurious standard as the bathroom, and it had been kept well. She caught herself wondering about who the former residents had been, back in the days before everything went belly up, and paperwork-based ownership ceased to exist.

So far so good, Elisabeth thought. The brothers were already happily lodged under her heel, but Eirin was a problem. Obviously, she couldn't just slit the redhead's throat or incinerate her or something equally quick and easy. Even though the brothers were letting their smaller heads do the thinking, they wouldn't be so addled that they'd fail to realize Elisabeth was the culprit. Fortunately, subtlety was her preferred way of doing things. Her glamour towards the same sex was likely a pale shadow of what it could be, had she practiced it more, but it should still be more than enough to seduce a simple farm girl. That in mind, she slipped back into her bathrobe, hoping she remembered what room Eirin was sleeping in

Finding Eirin's room didn't turn out to be a problem. It was the door covered with generous amounts of New Age bling and scribbles. Elisabeth almost laughed, looking at it. If the runes had been properly drawn, they would have protected Eirin against the War Witch's glamour. Alas, so close, and yet so far away. She shrugged, composed herself, and knocked gently on the door.

* * *

Eirin was tossing and turning. She'd performed the evening rite before going to bed, and couldn't remember if she'd done the pentagrams in the right order. She always messed it up at the end. Was it Water or Air that was the last one? Having Elisabeth constantly on her mind didn't make it any easier to concentrate either.

Eirin was no fool. She'd noticed the special status she got from being the only unattached female of desirable age for miles. Mostly, the menfolk were well-behaved, so she rather enjoyed the attention. Well, except for the incessant attention from Bjørn. Did the price of finding her inner wolf really have to be sleeping with that disgusting creature? The moon wasn't going away anytime soon, so she wasn't in that much of a rush, howling at it.

She shuddered at the thought of his flabby white skin. It wasn't just that he was ugly. It was obvious – even without wolf senses: his totem animal had to be the Rat. Besides, if he really was the revered teacher that he claimed to be, how come he'd managed to creep back here with his tail between his legs, without anyone hunting him? If he really had been the ceremony master of some stupid oasis, then no way they'd just let him leave. Even if the oasis had been bogus, he would've known who the members were. Information like that wouldn't be allowed to run free.

Still, that stuff didn't really matter. What really bothered her, was that Goth chick coming out of nowhere, challenging her position. And what a challenger! Eirin could almost forgive the brothers for falling for Elisabeth's wicked charms. She looked to be around Eirin's age – late teens – with a young and shapely body, curved in just the right places. Eirin compared it to her own slim, wiry and almost boyish body and unhappily accepted defeat. Add a perfectly oval face, with a mouth made for kissing, eyes to drown in, a petite nose and cheekbones distinct enough to give her face character. All of this framed by onyx black tresses. Even though Eirin didn't swing towards girls – as far as she knew – she might possibly make an exception in this case.

Just as she felt the first tendrils of sleep slither through the corners of her mind, there was a knock on her door. Furious, Eirin jumped out of bed, grabbing her robe on the way to the door.

'Fuck you, Bjørn,' she yelled, angrily tying her robe in place. 'Just as the gods intervened earlier, and made sure you didn't get any tail, you can be damn fucking sure that you aren't getting any now!' With a fierce scowl, she threw open her door – and came face to face with a somewhat bewildered, bathrobe-wearing Elisabeth.

'Eh…' The air went out of Eirin, the flush of anger replaced by the flush of self-consciousness. 'Sorry about that. I – um… I thought you were someone else.'

'Obviously. Sorry if I woke you, but one of you has been kind enough to hang my clothes up to dry, and I have no idea where!' Elisabeth smiled innocently.

'Yeah, those clothes shouldn't just be hung up to dry, they should be put away for good. Black lace isn't something any sane girl wears to the mountains! How long have you been on the run?' Eirin sighed, tilting her head. 'Ok, tell you what - since we're roughly the same size, you might as well borrow some more practical clothes from me. Probably a bit more down to earth than the kind of clothes you're used to, but I hope you can live with a t-shirt, a sweater and a pair of jeans. You'll be needing some underwear too, right?' Eirin was doing her best to cover up her embarrassment over her earlier outburst, and was close to babbling. 'But yeah, don't just stand there – come on in! We don't want to give the menfolk any funny ideas, do we?'

'So only it's the menfolk that get funny ideas?' Elisabeth answered with a laugh and entered. 'I've been on the run for a week now, and yeah, I'm getting a bit worn down,' she said, dropping down on Eirin's bed with a sigh. She lay on her back and stretched contently, letting her bathrobe slip further up her thighs. 'Sorry about all the bother I've been for you guys. I had no idea you were even out there.'

'Oh, no problem, shit happens. And I'm the one that should apologize, being so hostile towards you. It's not the kind of hospitality we usually pride ourselves on here in Myrvang.'

'No worries – if the roles had been reversed, I would have been much worse.' Elisabeth got up from the bed and walked over to Eirin. 'I know when I'm trespassing on somebody else's turf,' Elisabeth said as she gently took Eirin's hand. 'It can't be easy, being the only woman around. The brothers don't seem all that housebroken, to be honest, so I bet you have to do all the chores while keeping them at bay at the same time.'

A small voice in the corner of Eirin's mind was trying to raise an alarm. It was drowned out by the surprisingly nice feeling of Elisabeth's touch on her hand and the look of understanding and sympathy in those deep, beautiful eyes.

'It's not that bad,' Eirin explained. 'Tor and Geir have known me since I was a preschooler, so they don't look at me like that. And normally I'm not the only girl – usually we have 20-30 kids here. We school and train them to be able to take care of themselves in these fucked up times. There's a few of the girls that are a bit more open to Bjørn's... tutorship, and soon they'll be old enough for him to drool on them without being lynched. That's made him less insistent lately.'

'Bjørn's a clown,' Elisabeth sneered. 'Oslo was crawling with parasites like him. Like flies, they'd been attracted by the shit that was about to hit the fan, hoping to suck sustenance from it. And when it finally did hit, some profited, most perished – and only the true bottom feeders got away. Trust me on this. I've helped busting enough of those stupid lodges – or oases or whatever silly names the hippies use for their groups – to promise you that if he'd been involved with anything remotely serious, he would've been taken care of a long time ago. It's nothing I'm proud of, but we were thorough – no one with any real kind of knowledge got away.'

Elisabeth had gotten Eirin's attention now. This was the make or break moment, so Elisabeth put on her best puppy face, and carried on. 'The Church believes in training in the field, so we wannabe War Witches were sent out on our first missions pretty early. Who would suspect an innocent, sweet child of being an infiltrator? Of course, our enemies caught on – eventually. When mummy and daddy dearest started receiving packages containing bits and pieces of their protégé daughters, or movies of how they'd been killed, it caused quite a ruckus. A rule was made about parents being able to veto missions. Which was great for the girls from the important families. Not so great for the rest of us, since regular families were in deep enough shit with the Church as it was – for having a daughter tainted enough to be a witch – so they rarely dared provoking the holy fathers further. And with the pretty princesses relieved of frontline duty, it meant more missions for the rest of us.'

Eirin was listening intently, starting to feel utterly horrible about how she'd been treating Elisabeth. 'How old,' she almost whispered.

'Twelve. Or so I think, it's all a bit of a blur, to be honest. Later on, there were two years of training in a brothel, before I was sent here for my graduation.' Elisabeth answered with a shrug.

Eirin was aghast. 'You poor thing! So these are the monsters you're trying to get free from, stand up against, and defeat?' It was more than mere protective instincts that were awakening. She was intensely fascinated by this brave and crazy girl.

Elisabeth nodded, putting the statement that "body language can't lie" to shame. 'Enough about that. If I go into detail about the shit I've been through, neither of us will get any sleep. The important things is, I'm very grateful that you guys took me in. I wouldn't have had a chance by myself.' She squeezed Eirin's hand in gratitude, using the opportunity to draw Eirin closer.

Faced with Elisabeth's looks, Eirin underestimated her own beauty. In more civilized times, her mixture of strength, grace and good looks would have made her shine in a troupe of ballet dancers. True enough, she wasn't a classical beauty, with a thin, almost pointed face and a thick mane of deep red hair, occasionally hiding eyes that were burning with a fierce green fire. A bit skinny, but with a litheness and an animal magnetism that beamed sensuality, one could feel the wolf hiding under her skin.

Elisabeth looked into those verdant eyes, and with a soft voice she asked, 'What was it that you were so worked up about when I knocked on your door?' Their faces were so close that their noses almost touched.

Eirin flushed with embarrassment 'Well, um, I'm, like, supposed to be special. My mother is supposedly from a long line of mighty witches and shamans, and my father and his kin are said to have werewolf blood in their family. And according to some ancient prophecies the fruit of the union of those two bloodlines, meaning me, is destined to be some kind of hero or world saver. Problem is, I have the magical talents of a loaf of bread. No matter how much I study or train; nothing, nada, zilch. So, this summer, I went to this old woman who lives in the woods nearby – it's nothing weird, she's known me since I was a kid – and asked her for advice. She told me not to worry, and that it would all happen in its own good time. Usually, these things don't manifest until you're an adult and able to handle them, meaning I had to wait, in her own words, "until I become a woman". I was fool enough to tell this to Bjørn, and since then he has been relentless about getting med into bed to unlock my potential.'

The girls were looking intently into each other's eyes and had lowered their voices to throaty whispers.

'Bjørn's interpretation isn't completely off. There's usually some kind of sexual aspect involved when it comes to initiations,' Elisabeth admitted, allowing herself to be distracted by Eirin's gorgeous hair. 'But who says it has anything to do with penetration? Do you think the amazons were forced to rely on wooden dildos to unlock their powers?'

'But isn't a man and a woman the natural way of doing it,' Eirin asked curiously.

'The equipment used to get there has nothing to do with it. It's the mutual desire and the power in the orgasm that's the key factor. So, for instance, I don't think a rape would unlock anything. One person's lust isn't enough to transcend anything. Even though pain, rage and fear are powerful emotions, desire is much more primal and potent.'

'So, if I think that Bjørn is a disgusting sleaze bag, and only sleep with him out of duty, the sex won't have any effect?' Eirin's voice was hopeful, and she didn't mind at all that Elisabeth had started playing with her hair.

'Besides making you feel dirty and used? Not likely,' Elisabeth replied. 'These things are more like art than science. And you can't force good art. It takes inspiration, and most of the time it hardly feels like an effort at all – it just happens.' Elisabeth's hand had followed Eirin's hair to her scalp and was now gently caressing her chin and neck. Eirin sighed. Elisabeth's gentle, almost electric touch was something completely different from a man's rough grasp. She felt a lingering heat where Elisabeth had touched, spreading like fire through her body. A fire that exploded like a supernova when first lips, then tongues, met.

Elisabeth had had her share of rough sex, but Eirin took her by surprise when she threw her to the bed, disrobing her in the process. She let herself be pressed into the soft mattress as the frantic but inexperienced Eirin was squeezing and licking her enthusiastically, eager tongue focusing particularly on Elisabeth's erect nipples. As a domina she rarely experienced such raw and unbridled passion, especially in the form of a woman's touch, rather than the rough grip of a man. She closed her eyes, enjoying the sensations, caressing Eirin wherever she could reach. She guided Eirin's head towards her stomach while paying particular attention to Eirin's buttocks and inner thighs. Eirin got the hint and moved around so that she sat over Elisabeth, who noted with satisfaction that Brazilian wax-jobs weren't a fad out here. Body hair was considered sinful back where she came from, and there such a red bush would surely be seen as a portal to hell. Eirin continued kissing Elisabeth's thighs, letting out a small yelp when Elisabeth's tongue found its goal. She quickly returned the favor.

Entwined, the girls rolled around in bed, moaning. Eirin turned out to be a natural when it came to oral skills, and Elisabeth, not wanting to be outdone, started to use her fingers as well, bringing Eirin over the edge. With a scream, she locked Elisabeth's head between her twitching, surprisingly hairy thighs. Pleasure and oxygen starvation meant that Elisabeth had hardly noticed the hundred and twenty pounds of Eirin turning into six hundred pounds of hairy werewolf.

* * *

Meanwhile, at the foot of the small hill, Katherine was studying the cabins intently. Eager defenders had cleared the hillsides of any potential cover a long time ago - but that also gave any potential assailants an unobstructed view. After a while, she gave the binoculars back to Herlovsen. This was too easy. There had to be some kind of security system, or at least some hidden guards. But all she could Hear were five Voices, and everything seemed quiet. Good thing she had some mine sweepers. She flicked her wrist and pointed more or less at random at Designated Mine Sweeper Number One, Giske. 'You! Advance up that hill!'

Giske looked shocked. 'What? No fucking way! You can't just order me to my death! My father sits on the Council of Elders!' He had obviously forgotten where he was and who he was talking to.

Monkey grinned next to him, igniting a small blow torch he'd just pulled out of his pack. 'Would you like this up your ass instead, whelp?'

Giske swallowed hard and shook his head.

'Then I suggest you follow the boss's order and get said ass moving up that hill. First and only warning,' Monkey spat. 'Besides, that fancy armor of yours ought to protect you from shrapnel.' He looked thoughtful for a while. 'I wonder if they have anti-armor defenses. That would be worse for you. Anyway, get moving! You can only die once, kid, and you'd prefer it if it isn't at our hands.'

Giske threw Herlovsen one last, desperate look - then seemed to accept the inevitable. The others watched as he trudged up the hill - their faces lighting up as a mine exploded, throwing the young soldier sideways. Another explosion flared as he landed on a second mine, sending him flying again. Amazingly, the Italian armor had held, and Giske seemed mostly unhurt - at least physically. Mentally, on the other hand, there was room for improvement.

'You fucking cowards,' he screamed at the unseen enemy. 'Is that the best you can do?' Something snapped inside Giske and she started shooting wildly at some bushes before charging up the hill, gun blazing. 'Take that, you fucking fuck-faces! Feel the fucking fury of Christ!'

He'd gotten halfway up the hill when the jaws of a bear trap snapped shut around his leg. His battle armor saved his leg, but then the bent tree the bear trap was attached to sprung up. A steel wire pulled the trap – still clamped around Giske's leg – along with the springy spruce. His armor kept his leg from being torn straight off, but he went along for the ride, and with a perfect pendulum motion he smashed face first into the snowy rocks on the far end of the arc. He did not move afterwards.

'Good thing he was armored,' Erikka commented drily.

* * *

As the sirens started blearing and everything went flashing red, Elisabeth felt close to fainting from pleasure. Then, suddenly, the weight on top of her was gone, and she was just riding the aftershocks of orgasm when her survival instincts kicked in. That wasn't just any siren – that was an alarm sounding!

Eirin's instincts had been quicker, and she crashed through the door, her massive, furry shape sprinting down the corridor. She was on fire – in a good way. But, she could tell the fire would devour her if it wasn't sated; sated with blood. Eirin still had enough of a hold on herself to refrain from feasting on her friends – but the alarm meant intruders, and intruders meant dinner.

* * *

Bugger the element of surprise then, Katherine thought, and signaled to Diane to clear the way. This she did by starting to sing the same kind of howling, wordless song that she had sung before. Still in her man-wolf shape, she raised her furry head towards the moon and stretching her clawed arms out wide.

Herlovsen made a quick prayer for his soul as he noticed the wind picking up. Soon it was a storm, filling the air with snow blown up from the ground, and despite the extra weight of his armor, he had to grab hold of a nearby tree to keep on his feet.

Diane focused, gathering energy around her open palms, and when she was satisfied she had enough, she sent it up the hill in the form of two tiny tornadoes that crisscrossed their way up the hill, detonating mines and springing traps left and right.

'Herlovsen, you and your boys lead the charge,' Katherine ordered calmly. 'Stay away from the front door. The buildings are just made of wood, so we'll enter through a wall.'

Herlovsen had expected this. It was an old military tradition: if you by some chance ended up commanding soldiers from a different unit than your own, they were considered expendable. The grizzled sergeant and his three remaining boys moved out in triangle formation; Herlovsen on point and Bokalrud and Hoseth securing the corners. Berg was cowering in Herlovsen tracks, trying to make himself as small as possible.

Behind them, Katherine's crazies also went into combat mode. Diane swung one of her big, clawed hands and grabbed a metal-shod staff that had been strapped to her saddlebags. She whispered softly to it, and the metal bands on the ends started glowing. Ludvig remained in his saddle, but the dwarf had strapped a large energy rifle to it, and had just finished plugging in the power pack. Erikka was showing off her two antique Desert Eagles, while Harald was loading his crossbow. Monkey went for more modern weaponry, but had to change to his huge man-wolf shape to handle his 30mm autocannon. Katherine herself was inspecting her chains, attaching new end pieces to some of them.

All the airborne snow whipped up by Diane's storm made it impossible to see anything, so Herlovsen followed his navigation unit blindly, until the cabin wall loomed like a shadow just in front of him. They stopped, Herlovsen quickly placing a Can-Opener on the wall. He liked Can-Openers. The specially designed explosives had a singular purpose – making holes in walls – and were easy to use. Even his boys could do it. You simply attached it to the surface you wanted open, making damn sure that the correct side was facing inwards, yanked out the safety cord, pressed the button, and removed yourself to a safe distance. After a highly satisfying boom, the can would be open. At least according to the instruction manual.

With the boys watching, Herlovsen performed the can opening in perfect accordance with the manual, joining his squad behind cover – but there was a minor snag. What the instruction manual didn't include was a can-opening strategy an assault squad could turn to when the only thing separating them from a bloodthirsty werewolf was a solid log wall. Most specifically, it lacked points on what to do when said wall was no longer present…

* * *

The wall was gone, the air thick with smoke, and Eirin's wolf ears were ringing. But even if she was slightly dazed from the explosion, her reflexes were still fast as lightning. She was out the hole before the last wooden splinters had landed in the snow, going straight for the closest assailant. The sheer force of the attack made poor Bokalrud's armor worthless, the impacts shattering his ribs, bone shards perforating his lungs. He was already dead when she tore his head off with a vicious roar, and lunged to feast on the geyser of blood spurting from the stump of his neck.

* * *

The frenzied kill move was a rookie mistake that was about to cost the enemy werewolf dearly. The seconds it wasted on showmanship and eager gnawing on the corpse gave Herlovsen time to get it in his sights. He knew he'd end it - silver bullets or no silver bullets. Explosive rounds from an assault rifle at point blank range would reduce the beast to tufts of bloody hair, way beyond regeneration. He was just about to press the trigger and send the monster devouring Bokalrud's remains to doggie heaven, when Erikka knocked his rifle aside, shaking her head and mouthing a 'no'. Herlovsen looked confused as Monkey put his autocannon gently down in the snow, sprinted towards the gorging creature, and tackled it from the side. Obviously, werewolves came in different shapes and sizes, for the beast on the sergeant's side was at least a head taller and two hundred pounds heavier than the enemy one. The smaller abomination fought for its life, biting at Monkey's throat, but the bigger beast had it in a steel grip it couldn't escape.

* * *

Inside the cabin, everything was chaos. Fortunately, Tor had drilled them on what to do if this scenario happened. The plan was based on sound, well-tested principles - running away to be able to run away another day. Any hostile forces determined enough to stage this kind of attack would be suicide to resist. To this end, they had built plenty of escape tunnels, mostly hidden in the walls, leading to equipment depots stocked with everything they could possible need when fleeing; weapons, ammo, clothes, medical supplies, food and so on. Shit had a tendency to hit the fan at funny hours, so one might as well plan accordingly.

Elisabeth knew nothing about this, so she set out to follow Eirin, based on the simple theory that no matter what kind of gun toting psychos were out there, a berserk werewolf would be a more tempting target than an unarmed girl in a bathrobe.

Her new friend's tracks were easy enough to follow, and Elisabeth reached the hole in the wall just in time to see a huge, male werewolf tackle Eirin. Elisabeth reacted instinctively. She pointed at the man-wolf with her left index finger, while yanking one of the fire crystals loose from her necklace. As she crushed it in her right hand, a sickly yellow-green ray of fire struck the male in the back. His fur caught fire, bathing the whole scene in a sickly light. The shock made the brute lose his grip on Eirin, and she raked her claws across his sides before scrambling to her feet.

Despite her blood rage, Eirin realized she was badly outmatched. She felt a cool breeze at the back of her mind. Suddenly, she thought of her grandmother, and the thought soothed her enough to get her bearings. She saw Elisabeth standing by the hole in the wall, holding the enemies at bay with the same kind of fire that the big male she'd been fighting was rolling around to put out.

Tor's training sessions did their work, and her human side regained control. She dashed for the opening, yelling 'We flee!' She was already shrinking, almost back in human shape again, when she grabbed Elisabeth's arm and smashed through one of the false panels leading into the escape tunnels. Elisabeth had the good sense to let herself be pulled along, and as a metal plate swung down to seal the passage behind them, it seemed like they were safe for the moment.

* * *

Outside, Katherine and the hunters hesitated. For once, they were unsure about what to do. Elisabeth using hellfire? That was to be expected. A werewolf bodyguard? That was not to be expected. Diane was tending to the singed Monkey. His pride had suffered mortal wounds, but otherwise he was mostly unharmed. The others were waiting for orders from Katherine. She sent Erikka and Harald in to secure the cabin. It didn't take long before they returned, reporting back that the place was empty, but littered with tunnels. Their prey had escaped.

Katherine cursed and turned her attention to Herlovsen and Erikka. It was obvious that Herlovsen still fumed at not being allowed to shoot the other werewolf, but at least he was smart enough to keep a lid on it.

'We're hired to hunt the witch,' Erikka told Herlovsen matter-of-factly. 'Not our own kind. For your own sake, don't point any weapons at anything lupine while we're around.' She turned to Katherine. 'What now, boss?' she chimed perkily. 'And how's the kid?'

'The kid is fine,' Monkey growled, 'but I'm going to skin that fucking bitch and make a coat out of her when I get hold of her!'

'All in due time, kiddo,' Katherine said. 'And Erikka – you better get a grip on yourself. I don't want to see any more shit like that from you. You may see these soldiers as mere apes, but they're on our side.'

'Oh, for fuck's sake, Boss,' Erikka whined, feeling unjustly accused. 'He was about to shoot a werewolf! I'll never stand idly by and watch an ape waste one of us!'

Katherine sighed. 'Aren't you fur balls supposed to be able to regenerate or something? She would have been ok. Would you like to have Herlovsen here attacking you, the next time you're about to kill a human? Use your damned brain, next time.' Being human herself, Katherine had never tuned in to the racial loyalty the werewolves felt.

'I didn't attack him,' Erikka said defensively. 'He wouldn't be standing there if that was an attack!'

'It doesn't matter. I run the show here. If you aren't happy with that, you can run the fuck home.' Katherine voice cut like ice, but she knew she was pushing it. Erikka was an orphan as well, growing up with humans and having to come to terms with the fact that she was a werewolf all by herself. She was a bit touchy about not having a tribe or anything like that to back her up, so no wonder she instantly sympathized with a random, lone, renegade werewolf. Katherine had been playing with fire for a long time, leading the pack on her hunts. This pack was supposed to be the "Last Champions of Wolf Kind" or some bullshit like that, and even though she had dominated their leader in a fair fight, and thus gained leadership of the pack, she would be facing a mutiny if she forced them to stray too far from the fur balls' little Jihad. Practically speaking, she ought to be able to handle this hunt on her own. But, after hunting with these nutcases at her side for so long, she had to admit she'd grown a bit fond of them.

'Ok gang,' Katherine yelled. 'New priorities! Pay attention!' The pack gathered around her, interest in their eyes. 'We need to find out who the hell that werewolf is. Most likely an orphan that needs our help. She seems to be an associate of Elisabeth, so we're not giving up our hunt for that witch, but our first priority is to capture that werewolf – unharmed. Diane and Erikka – that will be your responsibility. And yes, you get to do whatever shit you need to, to accomplish that.' Katherine added the last sentence while looking at Herlovsen, hoping he'd get the hint.

Erikka seemed mollified by that, and they wasted no more time bickering amongst themselves.

* * *

While their attackers were arguing above their heads, the two girls scrambled through the tunnels like they had the devil himself hot on their heels. As they went, Eirin slammed and locked steel plate doors behind them that could buy them a few seconds, and armed vicious traps that would buy them more than a few seconds.

* * *

Of course, things had looked too simple just 15 minutes ago. Erikka had picked up one of the larger pieces of what used to be Bokalrud, and tossed it casually into one of tunnels. First, it just went splat on the floor – and half a second later, the explosion threw the charred remains back out.

'I don't think so,' Erikka said skeptically, turning towards Diane. 'Di, if you are done communing with your inner nurse, can you sniff out where the hell they've emerged?'

Diane stood and sniffed the wind for a few seconds, before she was off like a gray, almost invisible shadow. Harald was sent along as backup. The blonde Viking lookalike didn't seem all that comfortable, wading through the snow wrapped in winter gear, carrying loads of weaponry. He still wasn't all that comfortable in his wolf shapes – even though he'd never admit it – so he stuck to his human form as they set off on the chase.

* * *

The girls had paused to catch their breath and orient themselves. Now there was only one door between them and the winter night. The tunnels had deposited them in a storeroom, and Eirin started grabbing stuff from the shelves. She stuffed it into two backpacks, silently thanking Tor for anticipating this kind of scenario. Emergency rations, flashlights, and other survival gear. And a change of clothes. Alluring as it might be, being barefoot and naked wasn't all that practical when you were running away through the winter forest.

Eirin was double-checking the gear as Elisabeth suddenly cursed loudly. 'What?'

'God damn it,' Elisabeth exclaimed. 'I've forgotten my bag with all my stuff!'

'That sucks,' Eirin said impatiently. 'The tunnel is trapped, but you could always try to dodge through, give our new friends a hug, and pick up your bag along the way? Now get a move on!'

'You don't understand! All the things I need to keep the portal closed were in that bag!' Elisabeth sounded uncharacteristically desperate.

'Sweetie, unless we get our asses moving right now, we're never going to make it to the caves, not to mention to your precious portal!' Eirin had never been known for great patience and she half carried and half pushed Elisabeth through the door and out into the night.

The storm had blown over, and the low moon peeking through the dispersing clouds painted the surrounding spruces in a pale, calm light. The girls were far from calm, though, wasting precious time arguing. Elisabeth was desperate to get back to house to get her things, while Eirin steadfastly refused. Their raised voices sent a few crows flying off, looking for a quieter perch, and as the snow fell from the gently rocking boughs, Elisabeth arguments were cut short by a flash of green light that knocked them both to the ground. One of the crystals in her necklace had shattered, giving its energy to stop the crossbow bolt had been heading for her heart.

* * *

Harald stared in disbelief for a couple of seconds, shocked that some kind of force field had stopped his bolt, but snapped out of it as Diane charged by in her wolf-man shape, whirling her steel-shod staff.

Not wanting to be outshone, he drew his sword, Ice Tooth – a family heirloom that shone in the presence of evil. Right now, it bathed the whole area in daylight. The metal bands that shod the ends of Diane's quarterstaff were also glowing. It was a gentler and softer light, but looks can be deceiving – it could stun a mammoth. Diane preferred to avoid killing things – even devil spawn like

Elisabeth. Her shortcomings in that area were more than covered by the rest of the pack.

* * *

'Run,' Elisabeth roared in an inhuman voice, shoving Eirin away from the attackers while turning towards them, crushing several of the remaining crystals at once. Eirin stumbled away into the thicket of spruce as Elisabeth's eyes started shining with an evil, green light. She made two small, green balls of fire in her hands, and threw them at the charging, staff-wielding werewolf. They were easily deflected by some twirls of the staff, and then the beast attacked. Elisabeth jumped from tree to tree with unnatural nimbleness as the monster's staff blows reduced them to splinters. As she leapt and dodged, Elisabeth fired her small green bolts of fire. At first they didn't seem to do anything, but the more she flung, the slower the staff strikes rained down. Soon the werewolf had tired enough for Elisabeth to jump in close, land two punches in the furry stomach with glowing fists, and send beast and staff flying with a mighty uppercut.

Her intense focus on taking down the werewolf had made Elisabeth forget about the man. Big mistake. He had circled around and snuck up on her from behind, and was about to chop her in two with his brightly glowing sword. She noticed her shadow creeping, heard the crunch of snow under boots, and spun around with her arm raised in defense – just in time to see the bearded head explode, a cloud of blood and brains splattering all over her.

Tor lowered his rifle with a satisfied grin and motioned for the girls to follow him.

Elisabeth wiped her share of the blonde man's brains off of her face and took stock of the situation. The staff-wielding werewolf had gotten back on her legs, broken jaw apparently healed already, but instead of attacking again it had knelt beside the brainless man, cradling him while howling some weird song. Since it was not presently posing a threat, Elisabeth ran after Tor and Eirin. She had tried grabbing that fancy, day-bright sword along the way, but it burned her fingers badly, so she had to leave it behind. It didn't really surprise her that moon steel and hellfire didn't mix.

The trio heard the sound of engines from up ahead, and came quickly upon Bjørn and Geir, who had started their snowmobiles and had a third one ready for Tor. The girls jumped up behind them, and they roared off into the sunrise. Tor led the way, and for lack of options he steered for the Troll caves. All doubts about Elisabeth had been driven away by the attack.

* * *

Diane cradled Harald tightly. Suffering a headshot while in human shape put him in real danger of dying, and she was desperately stuffing brains – as well as a fair bit of snow and spruce needles – back inside his skull, while howling one of her healing songs.

Back at the cabins, Katherine and the rest of the pack had first heard the sound of trees splintering, then the shot, and then engines starting up and driving away. She assumed that Harald had messed up again, but it hadn't turned into a crisis yet. Elisabeth wouldn't be opening any portals until tomorrow night, so they had plenty of time to pick her up inside the caves.

Katherine ordered the pack to follow as she went to find out how the fight had gone. Once she got there, seeing the carnage, she cursed again. This was getting embarrassing. The last time two of them had been downed in a single fight, they'd been up against an entire clan of vampires.

Good thing she still had some cannon fodder.

* * *

The Troll Caves weren't that far away, just about a one hour snowmobile drive. The sun had started to rise, but this side of the mountain was still in shadow when they came to a large ravine. As they stopped to find a way to ascend, Eirin slid off the snowmobile and started throwing up. Geir ran over to her to help. She was crying, and the mixture of tears, snot and Bokalrud's caked blood made her look like a proper mess.

Geir tried to calm her down, but Eirin was near hysteria. The trip to the caves had been long enough to let her think about what had happened and what she had done.

'Stay away,' she cried. 'Don't touch me! I'm… I'm a monster! Oh, I can still feel the taste of his blood… And his flesh! Ooh f…' She threw up again. 'There's human flesh in my stomach! I killed… And… And ate somebody!' Geir was just holding her close, having absolutely no idea what to say.

Elisabeth was almost impressed. Considering what Eirin had been through, she was coping fairly well. It would be better for Eirin if she was allowed her reaction – that way she could get it out of her system – but Elisabeth didn't have time for such luxuries. She decided to use her powers instead, and mumbled some ancient words before stroking Eirin's hair gently, obfuscating the worst memories. They would reappear with a bang soon enough, but by then Elisabeth would no longer need Eirin – if the redhead even happened to live that long. It gave Elisabeth the tiniest flicker of a guilty conscience, doing this to Eirin, but then she reminded herself what was at stake, and finished the spell. Eirin stopped crying immediately, and was almost herself within a minute or two.

The caves were normally hidden behind a waterfall, but on a winter as cold as this, the waterfall had turned into a sparkling ice palace. This was a climb that was unsafe in the best conditions – and this wasn't close to the best conditions. Fortunately, there were iron spikes driven into mountain wall. Eirin played mountain goat, seemingly happy about being useful, and went on ahead, securing ropes the others could use. Tor went last, loosening the spikes as he passed them – a little surprise to anyone thinking to follow.

* * *

The Troll Caves weren't marked on any map or mentioned in any travel guides, but they were well known to local people. Somewhat awkward to get to, they went on for miles inside the mountain. If anyone had ever thoroughly explored them, they had taken that knowledge with them to the grave. Eirin was probably the person still living who knew them best, as she liked to wander off to explore and spelunk on her own. And she had only explored a few of the main branches that headed out from the large, moist cave just behind the waterfall. Whatever the geological processes were that had originally dug them out, they had clearly gotten some help from hands with opposable thumbs.

The caves showed clear signs of having been made more habitable, with ventilation shafts, supporting pillars and evened floors in many places. The rock was mostly sandstone, easily worked by whoever originally inhabited these caves. They had left traces of their presence not only by engineering, but also by weird markings in the soft stone. Some of the stick figures were fairly recognizable, but other shapes seemed more sinister. And although the script around the figures was indecipherable, the way they had been scratched into the cavern walls gave the dead language a harsh and rough feel.

It was surprisingly warm in the caves, and the further in one went, the warmer it got. The region had no volcanic activity or anything of the sort to explain the warmth. Eirin had brought a thermometer once, and according to it, the temperature was the same in the moist front cave as in the deepest parts she'd brought it to. Sure, the caves protected against wind, rain and snow, but no matter what the mercury said, it unarguably felt much warmer deep inside.

Nobody had lived in the caves since long before the Nailed God cursed the land. Well, not until recently. Some years ago, when the Church still believed their Cleansings would accomplish something, they were much more thorough, and ranged far into the countryside. When the people of Myrvang started seeing smoke from the direction of the neighboring village, they ran away and hid in the Caves while the Inquisitors cleansed any living thing they encountered. It was not a pleasant week. Trolls savor human flesh, and the thought of staying in one of their ancestral homes wasn't comforting, even though it had been long abandoned. They always had the feeling that there was something in the shadows, lurking. Something hungry. But the alternative, going out to face torture and death by fire, was even less pleasant. Nobody wanted to stay there longer than necessary, so as soon as their scouts confirmed that the Church's men were gone, the villagers had left the caves eagerly. Apart from Eirin – and Tor – very few people had been there since.

* * *

They half wriggled, half hacked their way through the ice, and emerged in the main cave. Elisabeth thought the frozen waterfall made the large cavity seem like a glittering cathedral. But, Tor pointed out that the ice was brittle, and the mouth of the cave was so large that the room wasn't all that defensible. Just crawling inside, hoping that they could remain hidden, would just be wishful thinking with werewolves sniffing at their trail. But, at least they could go somewhere more defensible - a somewhere Tor had already prepared. He led them through twists and turns, mostly upwards, and ended up on a ledge at the far end of a long, sloping gallery, where he'd built his very own survival bunker. He had fortified it with sandbags and gun positions, and stocked up with gas masks and provisions for half a year. He even had set up some portable beds. 'Sure,' he said, 'you can fire a weapon even if you're waist deep in wet mud, but you fight a lot better if you get some decent sleep.'

This cave lay a little higher than the others. Beside the tactical advantage that the passages leading to it sloped uphill, it also meant that it was easier to keep dry. Ventilation was a problem, so Tor had set up the diesel generators that provided electricity a few caves further in. CO_2 asphyxiation was a noobish way to die.

Tor had snapped back to battle mode and busied himself checking weapons, ammo and assigning guard duties. The others were comforted by him being seemingly in control of the situation, but Bjørn could see that Elisabeth was upset about something.

'What's up beautiful? From the way you are looking you'd think we were in the wrong caves or something,' he said, sitting down next to her.

'This is no joking matter,' she replied. 'I forgot the bag with my equipment back at the cabin. The things I need to keep the portal closed were all in it! It is hopeless now. All this is in vain! Tonight the portal will open and we will be overrun by demons!'

'Not if you're half as good as you claim to be, sweetie!' Bjørn grinned and dangled Elisabeth's bag in front of her. 'When everything started to blow up around us, I realized that you knew nothing about the escape tunnels. So, I went to your room to get you, but you weren't there. I saw your bag lying there, though, so I figured I'd rescue that instead. It might contain stuff that had sentimental value for you or something, since you were lugging it around.'

'How gallant,' Eirin commented with a scowl, but nobody heard her since Elisabeth shrieked with joy and threw herself at Bjørn, hugging him tightly.

'Then there's still hope, Bjørn! Oh I love you! You've saved me...us! All I... Um, all we need to do now is stay alive until we can do the ritual, and then...we've made it!' Elisabeth was kissing Bjørn all over, proclaiming her undying love for him.

Tor had assigned guard duties, and they were as prepared as they could be. Now they just had to wait – in the ancient, cavernous home of a race that had a fondness for human flesh. With an unsecured portal to Hell as their next-door neighbor. Not to mention the pack of rabid werewolves hot on their heels. The perfect setting to kick back and relax.

Tor put down a belt of ammunition in the left gunner's nest, and dusted off his hands. 'Well,' he said, cracking his knuckles, 'as long as those bastards can't move through solid rock, we ought to be able to hold them off for a few weeks. It's next to impossible to get heavy equipment up the mountain wall, and we've seen that bullets hurt them.' He seemed satisfied. 'I've done what I can, so what happens now is up to you,' he told Elisabeth. 'Any more preparations we need to do?'

'No, not you,' she said and smiled. 'I need to go through my book and prepare the rite. Lots of details to be memorized, but nothing that involves you. Just keep those damn mutts of my neck and we'll be good. Keep an eye on Eirin, though – she's been through some pretty heavy shit, and there's no telling how she'll react when she finally realizes that she's a murderous beast.'

Tor nodded and sat down next to Eirin. The redhead seemed calm but pale – at least in the parts of her face that weren't caked with Bokalrud's blood. He put on his most fatherly voice. 'You ok?'

Eirin met his gaze. 'Considering the circumstances, yes. I was never sure whether the stories and legends were true or not. Fair enough that the world had gone to shit, but parts of me were still hoping that Ingjerd was just telling fairytales. And now? Now I've torn out someone's throat with my own teeth... And do you know what the scariest bit was? The blood... and the feeling... It was delicious – and everything's changed now. I need help, Tor - help to find out who or what I am! And not the kind of help that your sleazebag brother Bjørn offers. I need to find my own kind! But... I have found them. And they're hunting us. Trying to kill us,' Eirin said softly, shoulders slumped.

'It was self-defense, sweetie. That soldier was there to kill you, and nobody will blame you for it.' Tor gave her a hug 'And besides – you still have us. We won't let anything bad happen to you.'

'But what about after we help Elisabeth save the world? Even with that portal closed, those psychos will still be outside, waiting for us.' Eirin couldn't shake the fear in her voice. 'I don't want to become a martyr!'

'We'll cross that river when we get there. Who knows, maybe we get lucky? Once they realize that they've failed, and the portal didn't open, they might just leave.' Tor didn't even sound like he believed it himself.

Eirin gave him a look. 'Yeah? I don't think so. After setting one of them on fire, tearing out a second one's throat, and blowing the head of a third? They'll want revenge.' She paused – swallowed. Her voice was breaking. 'Tor, were are going to die here. We may be able to take some of them with us, but no way are we going to survive this.' A tear glittered as it rolled down her cheek.

'Don't say that,' Tor said soothingly. 'Heaven knows what other tricks Elisabeth has up her sleeve. First we deal with the portal, then we worry about what happens next. You know how useless we men are when it comes to multitasking – we're no better at it when it comes to worrying,' he said, trying to make her smile. Subconsciously, Tor had started to see himself as a subordinate soldier again, and it was the job of his superior officer – Elisabeth in this case – to worry about anything besides surviving the next battle. 'And don't be too pissed off at Bjørn,' he added consolingly. 'He was only trying to help. It's not his fault that the knowledge of how to help someone awaken their inner werewolf is somewhat… um… esoteric and obscure.'

Eirin looked over at Bjørn and sneered 'Hah. The only thing he was trying to help was his own dick. Sometimes – especially when you are a blubbering fool, like him – it's better to leave things well enough alone! You can do a lot of harm if you have no idea about what you are doing. For instance, if a random person tries to perform emergency surgery, do you think he'll help or kill the patient? I could have respected him if he acknowledged his shortcomings, but he's just so… Ugh! So damned full of himself!'

* * *

Bjørn was too occupied with his own thoughts to pay any attention to Eirin and Tor. He had mixed feelings about this. It was all well and good that Elisabeth was grateful towards him; now that Eirin had gone sour, he might as well focus on getting in Elisabeth's good graces. But he still couldn't get the images he'd seen in her book out of his mind. He knew perfectly well that he was a fake. That was the first thing he realized about the Heimdal Oasis, once the shock of seeing a nude woman in real life had passed – it was all just a hoax.

Your average water polo team had more occult knowledge than them! It was just a scam to provide the leaders with cash, drugs and sex. A brilliant scam, actually. The suckered in lots of losers with no social life, and for the first time ever they got the opportunity to socialize with people just as messed up as them. Add some hefty dues for membership and initiations, mix in a generous helping of blind obedience, and a dash of ritual sex for good measure. It was the perfect deal.

Too bad the Church eventually caught wind of the operation and closed it down. He had to flee for his life, but he was such a lowly member that once he was out of sight, he was quickly forgotten. But his old dreams and hopes, that there had to be something more to life than mundane mediocrity, were not that easily forgotten. Even though all the losers like him, who wished for change, had gotten a lot more than they bargained for – and he kept hearing persistent rumors that the barriers between this world and other worlds had been torn down – he had never seen real magic. Not before last night.

When he collected Elisabeth's bag he had noticed the old, heavy grimoire inside. It was like the leather-bound parchment called to him. In the end, he hadn't been able to help himself – he pulled it out and leafed through the brittle pages while they waited on the scooters. He didn't understand much of what he saw. Given time, he could probably have figured it out, he told himself, but Auld English mixed with Latin wasn't his specialty – especially not when he had to read with the help of a flashlight.

The book was beautiful. Bound in thick, black leather, with fancy jewelry as clasps. The illustrations were magnificent and horrible, depicting various gruesome ways of sacrificing living beings. He couldn't care less about all the weird jewelry rattling about in the bag, but the book both excited and unsettled him.

So far, Elisabeth's story had turned out to be true. But how could he be sure that she was being honest with them about the portal? Those frightful illustrations seemed to indicate something opening, rather than something closing. Not that he could do anything about it if they were just brought along as sacrificial lambs. Not much he could do about that right now, though. He would have to talk things over with Tor. Those worrying illustrations were a secondary issue, anyway – the far more immediate matter was how to survive that pack of armed and raging werewolves waiting for them outside.

* * *

Said armed and raging werewolves were also busy setting up camp. Katherine was satisfied with having her prey cornered inside the Troll Caves. She knew about the rumored portal in there, as well as the auspicious time – and was pretty sure Elisabeth had the same information. There was no way to be sure it was really there, but Katherine wasn't taking any chances. That's why her plan was to strike at midnight, when Elisabeth was most likely to be busy with some elaborate ritual, trying to pry open this mystical gateway. What she didn't know, was Elisabeth's motives. Was she simply trying to use the portal to escape, planning to close it behind her? Or was the rouge War Witch on a quest of revenge, ready to flip the proverbial table by tearing the portal wide open and having hordes of demons swarm out to bring her burning vengeance down on the Church and everyone else on this God-forsaken planet? It was hard to imagine the six-year-old she had once known doing something like that, but Katherine couldn't risk it. There was more at stake now than her reward money.

By now, Elisabeth had a few hours head start. Based on the experience at the cabin, her annoying helpers would most likely have fortified the place quite well by now. Herlovsen was eager to strike immediately and have this all done with, but cooled his heels when Katherine agreed and suggested that the proactive sergeant could lead the charge himself. He actually considered it for a second – whether a quick death in battle could be an acceptable escape from this situation. He quickly figured that even if his body got perforated by sniper rounds, his soul would still be around for questioning afterwards; he might as well try to stay alive. So they waited.

Erikka was keeping their spirits up by messing with Monkey about how a burned Serb – amazingly enough – smelled even worse than a wet dog. Harald seemed to cope surprisingly well after his brain surgery, just a bit quiet, with an acceptable amount of drool discreetly shining in his beard. They spent the time discussing what they should focus on when they attacked. Erikka and Ludvig were adamant that the most important thing was to save the poor, confused werewolf girl and find a tribe for her. Katherine was most worried about maintaining their reputation. They'd already spent way too long on this, and it wouldn't look good if they had to follow their quarry literally straight to Hell. Diane pointed out that neither the werewolf girl nor their reputation would be important if they ended up with an open portal to Hell on their hands. Harald kept silent – but that was usual. He'd been utterly humbled when Katherine defeated him and assumed control of the pack. Katherine often pondered the wisdom of letting him stay with them. Very brave, and the first into any battle, his eagerness to prove himself almost made him a liability. Harald wasn't the original leader of the pack; that had been his father's honor. The role had passed on to him after pa got himself killed in battle. Secretly, Harald had been relieved when Katherine took over, as he knew he could never fill his father's shoes, but at least he'd managed to keep anyone from suspecting it.

Attacking during the ritual, disrupting it in the process, would make everyone happy. Diane was given the task of safely incapacitating the werewolf girl. Erikka and Monkey were to take out Elisabeth's other allies – but Elisabeth herself was Katherine's. The Cardinal would pay up a huge bonus if they brought her back alive, and Katherine didn't want to risk anyone messing up and inadvertently slaughtering the errant War Witch. While blood, guts, fire, bullets and tufts of fur were flying, it would be Ludvig's job to make sure the portal didn't open. Katherine thought Harald still looked a bit groggy, so he was assigned to stay in reserve, to step in when something unexpected happened. The sergeant and his two remaining toy soldiers were to charge in first, to draw attention and ammo. A battle plan as good as any!

The Troll Caves were a maze, with no maps available in any archive. Katherine thought it peculiar how Cardinal Mikkelsen just happened to have added detailed maps of these very caves among the documents he'd given her. Had he known this was where Elisabeth was headed all along? Something didn't add up – but she didn't have time to think about that now. She was certain the map was accurate, at least. She almost smiled, reminiscing over the accurate and very detailed map she had carved the back of the last fool to give her a bad map. After that, she never got inaccurate maps again. Sure, sometimes she didn't get maps at all – but when she did, they were always accurate.

As she looked over the immaculately detailed drawing, it was pretty obvious where the best defensive position would be – and where they'd find their prey.

* * *

Elisabeth was woken up by somebody shaking her shoulder. And what was that smell? Bacon? One look at Tor's face told her something bad had happened. She crushed one of her few remaining jewels, green fire reappearing in her eyes. Tor motioned for her to keep silent and follow him. He led her further out towards the exit, where the smell was getting stronger. It wasn't really bacon. No, something sweeter. Something nauseous.

Someone had lit a fire in the vast cavern behind the waterfall. Shadows danced with glittering orange light among the shiny spires of the ice palace, and as they made their way out of the dim tunnel, Elisabeth saw the source of the smell. It was Bjørn.

It was like a bizarre spit roast. Someone had stripped Bjørn naked, gagged him, and pierced him with a metal bar from his ass to his mouth. And not only that; he'd been bent in a way that made the bar exit the small of his back and re-enter his head just under his skull. With his arms and legs strapped to the bar with thick, barbed wire, the piercing wounds had not been immediately lethal. It was likely he had still been alive for some time while being roasted. Weird sigils had been carved into his skin, the bleeding lines made to pop by the searing heat.

'Fuck' was all Elisabeth managed to say before her vomit splashed wetly on the rocks. Wiping her mouth, she had a dawning suspicion about what had happened. And what was worse, the ritual for opening the portal required five participants. Even though they were supposed to be sacrificed towards the end, they all had to be alive at the beginning. Corpses didn't count! So close, yet so fucking far away - and all because of her own sloppiness! Of course she'd protected her stuff from snooping eyes with some demonic curses. She wouldn't have given it a second thought if one of her fellow witches-in-training died horribly, so she hadn't bothered to put any upper limits as to how harshly the curse should strike. Bjørn had been too curious for his own good, and since she hadn't deactivated the curses, he had obviously triggered them. Such a shame. Even though he was a bit of a pig, he seemed like a fairly decent fellow. Not someone who deserved to die so horribly! And she didn't deserve to have her plans unraveled over a detail like that! She pressed her lips together with frustration. Maybe a werewolf counted as two people?

'We'll have to mourn and bury him later,' Tor whispered, interrupting Elisabeth's train of thought. 'We're not alone here. And all that matters now is to stay alive for the hours you need to keep that portal closed.' Elisabeth was almost shocked at how cold and mechanical Tor had become – his lizard brain was definitely back on the battlefield. She'd only seen this kind of detachment in commandoes operating behind enemy lines for months at a time. Elisabeth was getting really curious about where he'd served. But, those questions would have to wait until they survived this mess, and she put it among the other loose ends that would have to be dealt with later.

Tor and Elisabeth took the corpse down from the spit, packed it in plastic, and put out the fire before it ate all the oxygen. When he went back to get the plastic, Tor just told the others that somebody had struck while they were sleeping – and killed Bjørn. Whomever it was could probably have killed the rest of them as well, but since they were still breathing, there probably wasn't any present danger of attack at this very moment. Still, he told them to be alert.

Tor realized that the last thing they should do was to get bogged down with their own dark thoughts. So, even though the thought of eating made his stomach turn, he made sure the others were occupied making food. While they ate in silence, he mentally went over their strategy. This place might be the best place to fortify – but they weren't just here to save their own skin. The portal was the key – and that's where they had to make their stand. It was time to move camp.

It was a large cave, almost the size of a hockey rink, but it only had one narrow tunnel leading to it, an easily defended choke point. Two of them stood guard in the outer cave, while two were lugging gear into the inner cave, swapping places regularly to keep a quick pace. It didn't take them long to relocate and set up new defensive positions. When everything was in, gun nests and all, Geir and Tor mined the passage. Only anti-personnel mines though - Tor didn't want to collapse their only exit.

For a normal person, there didn't seem to be anything special about the portal cave, other than its size. Elisabeth, however, sensed immediately that this was the place. She got to work right away. She needed some time to prepare, especially now that she had to change the rite to work with four people instead of five.

She took out a large piece of black cloth, laid it out on the cavern floor, and drew a pentagram on it with a stick of chalk. In the middle of the pentagram, she placed a couple of Tor's ammo crates. Once she had draped a red altar cloth over them, they looked the part. Then she broke open the tattered plastic on a large, old box of candles from IKEA, placing them around the pentagram in a seemingly random fashion. Once she'd laid out all her assorted ritual paraphernalia, she took a step back and surveyed the scene. Her main problem was that the rite required five people, one at each arm of the pentagram. The five-pointed star was supposed to be surrounded by a warding circle, and that would take five people to maintain. Which they were not. She sat down with her grimoire to memories the chants and to try and see which point of the pentagram was the least important, and could be dropped. As she traced the sigils on the cover they began to glow and she heard a familiar rasping voice inside her head

'You call, boss?'

'Ghurlax,' Elisabeth thought back at the book's demonic guardian; 'you useless piece of shit! You've fucked it all up! How am I supposed to open the portal with only four participants?'

'I'm so sorry boss. Just following your instructions,' the demon answered smugly. 'Anyone tampering with your things is to be killed according to his or her own inner nature. This time, roasted pig seemed highly appropriate.'

'I've never instructed you to be an idiot. I thought you demons were supposed to be crafty and devious!' Her thoughts oozed of disappointment. 'You know you'll never get back to Hell if I don't get there myself.'

'To be honest, boss, I have to admit that we demons might be a bit overrated. Marketing, you know. At least we do that right! And don't you worry about Hell. I've got a hunch we'll get there in due time.' The demon sounded amused. 'Besides, what's all the fuzz about? You know perfectly well that the pentagram and candles are just trappings. And the amount of blood? That doesn't matter either. As you are well aware, one tiny drop of your own precious ichor is worth buckets of sacrificial blood. And don't forget you have a werewolf, too, boss! Her soul ought to count for way more than the exact number of brothers you sacrifice.'

'Isn't there any other way to open that damned portal? These people have been good to me.' She hadn't expected it, but Elisabeth's conscience had been gnawing at her for a while now. 'They deserve a better fate than having their souls devoured to open a portal.'

'Sorry, boss, but this isn't exactly a stroll down Sesame Street. Believe it or not, the trolls knew what they were doing. The shaman sacrificed his five innocent little children to seal the portal, so obviously we need some pure souls to open it again. I guess that was the theory – anyone actually wanting to open that portal would be hard-pressed to find enough pure people to sacrifice.'

'And my new companions,' Elisabeth asked 'are they supposed to be pure?'

'Well, you know them better than me, boss! The roasted pig didn't seem particularly pure, I'll tell you that. The others? Close enough, I guess, close enough. Only one way to find out for sure, though! At least I carved the sigils into the pig's flesh before grilling him, so even if you're not going to eat him, keep his remains close by – he might still count, and not go to waste. You might as well just try the rite, boss. Whining doesn't become you.' Ghurlax was taking liberties, making Elisabeth frown, but the leather bound demon continued, unabashed. 'It's not like you really have a choice, boss. I mean, you could head out and ask Katherine to help. Maybe she could volunteer one of her wolves as a stand in? That could get interesting. Oh, cheer up, boss - you apes worry too much!'

Elisabeth cursed. She was envious towards white magicians. A guardian angel must be so much easier to deal with than a guardian demon. Especially a guardian demon that actively misinterpreted her orders, just to spite her. How far could she trust Ghurlax? What did she know about the damned little imp? Not much, honestly. She didn't even have any idea of how it looked. She only knew it as a voice, trapped in a book, making shit happen. In nasty ways. It seemed to always follow her instructions to the letter. Like most ambitious War Witches, she had secured the services of a guardian and servant in exchange for bartering away her soul. She didn't even know who or what she'd made her deal with – all she'd been told afterwards was that Ghurlax would take care of any further communication. Elisabeth wondered briefly about just how powerful Ghurlax really was. It must have conjured that spit from somewhere, and overpowering Bjørn without waking any of them would have taken more power than she'd thought Ghurlax had. Most likely it was playing her for a fool – but that was to be expected when dealing with demons.

Elisabeth forced herself to think about more pressing matters instead. She decided that putting Bjørn's corpse where he should have been standing might work. She'd have to drop most of the protective circles, but that part was, strictly speaking, only relevant if you summoned a single demon that you wanted to control. Throwing the Gates of Hell wide open would make simple circles of protection pretty irrelevant.

With a bout of inspiration – and, frankly, guesswork – Elisabeth finished creating her Open Portal to Hell Ritual, Version 2.0, wrote down the words the others were supposed to chant, and went over the details with them. None of them had participated in ritual magic before – and none of them had ever imagined themselves sitting in a cave, chanting weird words around a pentagram, but now they were too deep in it to even think about objecting. Elisabeth realized the fear and sorrow that Bjørn's killing had induced would actually be beneficial, the extra layer of emotion making the ritual easier to perform for her conjurers-in-training. They hadn't even complained about having Bjørn's dead body at their side. Maybe Ghurlax had known what he was doing after all? Oh, demons! How unsearchable are their judgements and how inscrutable are their ways!

* * *

Outside, the werewolf pack was busy as well. Katherine's plan of striking during the ritual meant that they had to prepare for a pretty unpleasant eventuality: they could be facing an open portal to Hell. Herlovsen and his two surviving soldiers were informed that ordinary weapons would have no effect on demons. Luckily, Katherine's chains, Diane's staff and Erikka's heirloom guns were far from ordinary, and Ludvig and Diane were already occupying themselves with the insanely tedious job of blessing every single bullet for the regular guns.

In case they failed in their efforts to keep that portal closed, necessary warnings and instructions were written and put in the saddlebags of the hounds. The beasts would wait loyally outside, ready to chase down any lone escapees, but they had enough sense to flee if a horde of demons started to pour out of the caves, and they knew where to go. Katherine felt better knowing those messages would at least give some people a chance to put up some kind of defense against the demons before the whole Scandinavian Peninsula was overrun.

Katherine assumed the mountain men would have booby-trapped the tunnels by now, and a quick peek from Erikka confirmed her suspicions. Good thing she had Herlovsen. Time for the toy soldiers to shine! After a vivid description of the consequences of disobeying orders, Herlovsen agreed to the wisdom of the plan and prepared to lead Hoseth and Berg up the passage. It was easy to get both boys to agree that being blown up by a mine was infinitely better than being devoured by a demon.

* * *

It's amazing how slowly time can pass when you are waiting for the possible end of the world. Both groups went into action about one hour before midnight.

Elisabeth had designed a very elaborate rite. She tried to compensate for not really having the proper paraphernalia by adding lots of chanting and drawing of sigils. Besides, rushing it with so inexperienced practitioners at her side was an invitation to disaster.

Katherine, on her side, didn't want to time things too closely. Her plan seemed to work well, at least in the beginning. With Herlovsen in front, the armored trio carefully made their way through the passages, detonating explosives as they passed, shrapnel and pebbles bouncing off their Italian suits as expected.

Elisabeth could hear the distant explosions, but didn't let it distract her. The attack was expected, and she had designed the rite accordingly.

The first part was all about blessing the chalice that would hold their blood. Ideally, the chalice would remind the practitioners of the Holy Grail, or would be the skull of some sentient being, but in a pinch, simpler chalices could be acceptable. Elisabeth had gone for a plastic cup, and Tor was the first to cut his arm and let his blood bleed into it before returning to his post, guarding the entrance to the cavern. The rest of them used Elisabeth's athame – a black-handled ritual dagger – to cut themselves in turn, and soon the cup was filled. The rest of the ritual had to be performed by only three chanters. Five would have been ideal, but these were far from ideal circumstances, and when she had redesigned the rite, she'd been clever enough to make a few practical considerations.

Elisabeth promised herself that if she survived this mess with her soul intact, she would retire and spend her autumn years writing "Black Magic: A Field Guide for Dummies". Way too many rituals were designed by daft armchair magicians. Like, how the hell were you supposed to find the six hundred and sixty-six virgins required for some rituals? Not to mention the logistics of finding a place large enough to hold over six hundred and seventy people. You'd need to hire a bloody event company to pull that off! It would have been nice not having to start from scratch every time she had to design a ritual to use in the field. As Elisabeth drew the sigils that activated the different elements, Geir and Eirin would need to chant to maintain the connection. Normally, there would one chanter for each element, but in the current situation each of them would have to do the job of two. Once that was done, Elisabeth had to mark the sacrifices – or, "bless the anointed," as she said. She went around the circle, carefully using the tip of her athame to draw sigils on the skin of the others. The dagger was so sharp it didn't really hurt, even though she drew blood, and neither Geir nor Eirin noticed that the symbols were exactly the same that they'd found carved into Bjørn's dead body.

* * *

The pack was making good progress through the passages. Herlovsen and his men were up front, dashing through the detonating booby-traps. They stayed mostly unhurt thanks to their Italian battle armors. The suits were turning out to work surprisingly well now that they were in a non-arctic environment. They passed through the caves where their prey had slept, thankful they didn't have to face anyone manning those fortifications, but when they closed in on the portal cave, they were met with a hail of gunfire. Only their armor gave them time enough to throw themselves back into cover. The easy progress had made them a bit overconfident, the suits making them feel almost invincible, so Herlovsen ordered Berg to ignore the spray of lead and lead the charge. Berg had no option but to follow orders, so he charged bravely.

The running soldier collapsed screaming and gurgling as the unseen defender placed a bullet in each of his fairly unprotected kneecaps. Nobody felt particularly keen on rushing forward to help. Judging from the amount of blood gushing out, they knew that Berg would stop screaming soon enough.

'That was pretty accurate shooting, boss,' Erikka said, a master of stating the obvious as always. 'This'll hurt.'

Katherine cleared her throat. 'Ludvig? Do you have anything in your bag of tricks that might help?'

'Sure thing, Kat' the dwarf said and took a box out of his saddlebags. 'This ought to prove fun!' He grinned and revealed what looked like a grenade-sized Easter egg. 'As long as we don't drop it on the floor. Throw this little baby as far up the tunnel as you can; that ought to give us enough cover,' Ludvig said and handed the egg to Katherine

* * *

Even though the caves had become quite cold, Elisabeth had broken into a sweat. She was almost ready to open the gate. Red streaks ran from the sigils she had carved into the skin of the chanters, and the plastic "chalice" loomed on the altar in the middle of the pentagram, pregnant with powerful blood. She started to invoke the name she had found in the grimoire, hoping her pronunciation wasn't too far off.

Suddenly, a large ball of greenish fire appeared over the cup. It was a cold fire; unnatural flames that sucked up all warmth. Even the beads of sweat on her forehead froze. Geir was holding up his candle, standing there with clenched teeth, like a statue, stubbornly focused on doing his part. The other candle holder was much less like a statue. Eirin was pale and her arms were shaking visibly as she struggled to hold her IKEA candle up. The other three candles sputtered and went out.

Eirin gasped as a flaming tentacle emerged from the green fireball, its tip plunging into the cup to consume the blood. They stared as it rose from the empty container, drunk with power. With a loud, wet noise, the tactile member split into five appendages. Three of them started floating towards those in the circle, one hovered over the body of Bjørn, and one snaked towards Tor, who was oblivious to what was going on behind him. A large white oval appeared on the cavern wall.

'Ghurlax! What the fuck is going on?' Elisabeth was getting worried. If that was her portal, it had the wrong color. Right now it seemed to lead to some bright and shiny place where she probably wouldn't be welcome at all.

'Don't worry boss,' the rasping voice echoed in her head. 'The portal is neutral at the moment. It's active – but it isn't set for any destination. That's what we need to do next - set it for the nice and warm place we're going. Let's hope that's what the demon you just summoned is here for.'

'Hope? You goddamned gnome, you fucking house elf, hope has no place in Hell!' Elisabeth was furious – and very, very scared. 'I can't control this thing! We only have moments left before it sucks up all of our life forces!'

It almost seemed like the glowing oval reacted to her rage and fear. The whiteness took on a sickly greenish tinge. Elisabeth searched her brain, trying to dig up half-forgotten textbook knowledge about portals. She remembered that most of them were locked between two specific spots in two specific worlds, and over time begun to mimic the appearance of the places they led to. Others were only anchored on one end, and could in principle be used to go anywhere – you just had to set the destination. If you knew what you were doing, that destination would be somewhere with another open-ended portal, so you could get back. Of course, you didn't have to know what you were doing. You could jump blindly, if you were willing to risk ending up inside a volcano or at the bottom of an ocean – something most people found rarely advisable. So, the question was: how do you quickly set a destination for a portal?

In theory, all it took was a strong will and a clear picture of the destination. Easier said than done. Any distractions causing wavering in the image or other defects could send your atoms scattered all over the multiverse. It was better to have some kind of navigational aid, like some powerful item strongly attuned to the place one was going. Elisabeth didn't have that. What she did have, was some powerful energy from the destination – that could work as well. A fire demon, like this cold-burning tentacle thing, was almost pure energy. The question now was whether she had it, or it had her.

While she was forming a plan, the tentacle had enveloped her. The sigils worked – attracting it, but protecting her with a mystical field at the same time, so it couldn't directly touch her. It wrapped itself around her like a cocoon, the same way the tentacles that had been heading for Geir and Eirin did. Fortunately, the two didn't panic. The cold was intense and physically painful. The tentacle heading for Bjørn's corpse was hovering over it, hesitating like it was in two minds about the matter, before it was suddenly sucked back into the green ball of flame with a swoosh. The orb of fire started pulsating, the flames changing color from green, going through the spectrum towards orange and red. The four remaining tentacles seemed more agitated, almost as if the eldritch thing had become angry.

Elisabeth started feeling less cold, almost warm and cozy. That was a bad sign – she knew she had just moments to live and struggled towards the portal, planning to make the tentacle wrapped around her touch the shimmering surface. But the portal seemed so far away. She was so incredibly tired; all she wanted to do was to lie down and sleep – just for a little while – but she gritted her teeth and struggled on, step by step.

The portal was shining more strongly, almost as if it was aware that it was about to be used. Out of the corner of her eye, Elisabeth noticed that something was thrown into the cavern. She didn't have time to think about it further before it exploded with nauseating gas, the shock wave throwing her off her feet.

Fortunately, the explosion had pushed her in the right direction. She could see the portal in front of her, shimmering through the smoke. The cave was ringing with the loud noise of an assault rifle on full auto. Tor was obviously busy emptying his magazine down the passage. At least the horrible gas stung her eyes enough to wake her up, and she staggered the last few steps towards her goal, pulling her fiery tentacle to its fate.

As Elisabeth reached the portal, she raised her hand, making the fire demon's tentacle come into contact with the shining oval. A sputtering noise filled the cave. The portal flared into a kaleidoscope of colors, and the fire demon was sucked into it, tentacles pulled loose from all of them – before the colors settled down. The portal went back to shining white again.

'No!' Elisabeth screamed, beating her fists against the portal, which had turned hard, smooth and unyielding.

'Well, that was an unfortunate setback, boss,' Ghurlax' voice rasped in her mind. 'It would appear the fire demon wasn't powerful enough. I believe this proves it would have needed the energy of five beings, not four – werewolf and prodigy blood notwithstanding.'

'You don't say, Ghurlax,' Elisabeth thought icily. 'Maybe I should toss your useless tome into the portal and see if it helps!'

* * *

Harald and Monkey had had a long argument about which one of them had the most right to feel aggrieved, and thus had the biggest claim on the right to throw the egg – the weapon that Ludvig promised would break the defense. Katherine quickly grew tired of their bickering, so she told Monkey to throw it. She couldn't be sure the still-drooling Harald wouldn't fumble yet again and detonate it at their feet. And Monkey had military training, so he should know how to handle a grenade-like weapon. At least in theory…

Monkey used a mirror to aim, before rolling around the corner and throwing the egg in one swift motion. It was a perfect throw, the burly Serb so fast that he was back around the corner before the gunner inside could draw a bead on him.

Herlovsen and Hoseth knew their job and charged up the passage as soon as they heard the thunder of the explosion. An assault rifle roared on full auto, and Herlovsen felt the impact of several bullets hitting him straight in the chest. He was thrown to the ground, but the armor held. Hoseth was dazed by a couple hits as well, and the two prone soldiers were simply run over by Katherine and her pack. Having done his job as an expendable human shield, Herlovsen followed them as discreetly as possible. Herlovsen's only long-term hope of survival was to see so much interesting shit that his report would convince his superiors to let him live as a reward.

* * *

It was just as well that the smoke covered what was really going on by the portal. Elisabeth had convinced her helpers that she was trying to keep the portal closed, but not even the most love-struck, naive fool would have believed that if they had seen how she was screaming and pounding at it.

After the explosion, Geir had thrown himself to the ground, drawn his gun and was trying to crawl towards what he thought was the exit. Eirin's self-control had snapped – she had given in to panic and started changing into her hybrid form. With her heightened senses, she noticed large shapes bounding toward them through the fog, and threw herself at them with a snarl.

The assailants obviously saw her coming. The staff-wielding one told the others to back off, and decked Eirin with a solid blow from her weapon. Eirin flew through the cavern before hitting the wall with a soft thud, collapsing in a paralyzed heap.

The chaos was complete. The sound of shooting echoed off the cavern walls, while the thick, acrid smoke made everyone blind. It was just like the enemy wanted it. The pack seemed to be a well drilled killing machine that leapt into action with no need to see or hear each other to coordinate their attacks.

Elisabeth more felt than saw Eirin hitting the wall next to her, and Tor was no longer shooting. It seemed the battle was already lost. She was trying to come up with something she could use to bargain with Katherine. After all, her bounty hunter wasn't one of the whores of the Church, so all hope wasn't lost. She had turned her back on the portal, leaning on the glassy surface while preparing for the speech of – and for – her life, when all of sudden her support vanished. She tilted backwards, but didn't fall far before she was bowled over from behind by something huge leaping out of the portal, knocking her straight to the rocky floor.

She was a bit dazed, but in the light from the portal Elisabeth could make out a huge shape. It was the size of a grizzly, smelled far worse than a grizzly, and had a huge club or axe in its hand. It was quickly followed by several other creatures coming through the portal. Reinforcements – but for whom? The second being through was clad in old fashioned plate armor, like some archaic knight, and had entered with a much too graceful combat roll, considering its cumbersome mail. More followed, some armored, some not - but Elisabeth was much too busy finding a way to survive to bother counting heads.

* * *

Katherine was supervising the chaos, satisfied that things were going like she wanted, when she saw the shapes coming through the gateway. She blinked – she recognized that armor! Getting a second look, she realized this could be none other than her old comrades, Constansa and Theresa. The huge one must be Cullen – and the rest she couldn't care less about. She wasn't pleased to see them, for their parting of ways had been far from amicable. During the last battle of the war, Constansa had sacrificed part of her forces to act as a diversion. Katherine had been leading that diversion, and was somewhat miffed about being sent to her death without being told.

Also, the timing of them showing up now? It was beyond ridiculous. Katherine thought Constansa's guardianship of Elisabeth had ended when she handily forgot all about her promise to return and check up on how the prodigy was doing, but this sudden appearance was Constansa's modus operandi – popping out of nowhere to wreck even the most well improvised plan.

There were a lot of battle-hardened psychos in the cavern right now, and most of them were acting on pure instinct. Herlovsen, Hoseth and the guy entrenched in the gun nest stopped shooting at each other and opened fire on the shapes coming out of the portal instead. They were mostly hitting the walls, with bullets ricocheting all over the place, but at least one of the shapes dropped.

Katherine thought Constansa and Theresa wanted to be better safe than sorry, for suddenly their swords and armors leapt into flame. She knew that made them impervious to bullets and other ordinary weapons, but on the other hand, made them stand out as targets. Another of Constansa's party – it might be the one called Baz – had produced a large umbrella, which he opened. It seemed quite bulletproof, and he hid himself and their fallen comrade behind it.

Harald, who felt he had something to prove, changed into hybrid shape and leapt at the newcomers with a snarl. He landed straight in front of Cullen, who smiled when he saw that he was facing a werewolf and didn't have to pull his punches. He didn't – and Harald collapsed like a bag of potatoes. Erikka was more experienced, and as Diane and Theresa began an impressive light show where a glowing staff clashed with a flaming sword, she changed into her half-wolf shape and snuck up behind Baz, who was busy positioning his bulletproof umbrella and didn't notice her before she struck. The material might well have been bulletproof, but the stick itself was ordinary wood and Erikka quickly chewed it to splinters. Baz was weapon- and defenseless, and before he could come up with some other gadget, Erikka head-butted him out of the fight.

Katherine was whirling her chains a shield as she approached the other flaming figure. 'Constansa! Long time no see, my dear! How nice of you to drop by. But you can piss off now! Elisabeth is mine. Your custody ended when you failed to protect her to begin with!'

Constansa whirled in the direction of Katherine's voice and advanced with her sword drawn and murder in her eyes. 'Katherine, you filthy traitor – keep your damned tentacles off her! I will not let the prodigy of our age become a pawn of Hell!'

* * *

'I'd prefer not to be a pawn of you angel lovers, either,' Elisabeth muttered to herself, keeping her head down as bullets and harsh words were flying over it. Just when you thought things couldn't possibly get any worse. Being recaptured by a corrupt Church would be pleasant, compared to being saved, purified and rehabilitated as a Foot Soldier of Heaven.

Katherine and Constansa clashed furiously. Constansa seemed hampered by holding something looking like a crown or tiara of sorts in her left hand – her lack of grip meant she couldn't use her shield properly. Katherine had noticed this and naturally went for the crown with her chains. She managed to snag it, but Constansa countered by severing the grasping chains. The crown went flying wildly through the air, landing straight in front of Elisabeth. Around them, the grand melee had broken down into several smaller fights. Eirin, Harald and Baz were down. Erikka was keeping Cullen busy by jumping around and dodging his powerful but slow attacks without too much effort. Theresa and Diane were evenly matched, and victory would come to the one that tired last. Tor had realized that shooting blindly was doing him no good, so he'd brought out a first aid kit was crawling along the floor, trying to help his allies in any way he could. It had all become too much for Geir; he just lay curled up in a fetal position, moaning. And Herlovsen and Hoseth were crouched low, backs against the cavern wall, hoping they'd been forgotten.

Ghurlax's rasping voice came out of nowhere, like usual. 'Pardon me, boss, but you might want to make a quick acquisition of that crown, as it were. I believe it to be the Crown of Potential, which should easily open the gate to where ever we want.'

'I'm going to regret this,' Elisabeth groaned, 'but do I have a choice?'

'Not if you want to live, boss.'

The crown didn't look impressive at all. Simple and made out of a single piece of gold, it was a slender headband with a lone spike standing straight up, its tip adorned with a jewel. It looked as if it was designed to be easily knocked off of the wearer's head.

Elisabeth tried moving her aching limbs. Feeling that nothing important was broken, she dove like a snake for the crown.

* * *

Without the crown to worry about, Constansa was back on an even footing with Katherine.

'We would have sacrificed ourselves willingly if you'd told us the truth,' Katherine shouted as she tried to entangle Constansa's sword with her chains.

'There were spies among us,' Constansa spat through gritted teeth, shaking her sword loose. 'If I'd told you the truth about the charge being a diversion, the sacrifice would have been pointless!' Constansa let Katherine's next strike entangle her sword and sword arm. She yanked hard on Katherine's chains, trying to disarm her, but the chains were built into Katherine's armor, and Constansa simply pulled her opponent towards her. Katherine used the momentum to attack with the vicious spikes that had suddenly sprung from both her fists. When Constansa swerved out of the way, Katherine swiped with her legs, knocking Constansa to the ground.

There was no sense of fair play in this fight. Katherine pressed her advantage on a lying Constansa, who rolled nimbly away and countered with a blast searing blast of fire. That sent Katherine back on the defensive and gave Constansa time enough to get back on her feet, flaming sword at the ready. Constansa saw Elisabeth's movement from the corner of her eye, but had to keep her focus on her opponent. Katherine was circling, using her chains as whirling shield while looking for an opening.

'Sacrifice! That's your damned fetish isn't it?' Katherine spat at Constansa. 'Just because you lost that pampered life you think you were meant for, you think you can go and make the decision for everyone else, huh? Just how many lives have your choices destroyed over the years?'

Neither of them could break the other's defenses, and they could probably have kept fighting and bickering until the end of days if it hadn't been for Elisabeth reaching the crown and putting it on her head. It had seemed a bit large for her when she first picked it up, but as she put it on, it felt like it shrunk a bit. Not enough to make a tight fit, but enough that she didn't have to hold it in place. Putting it on felt like a rush of drugs. First an electric shock, followed by a pleasant warmth and a feeling of confidence spreading through her. She stood up, feeling refreshed, looking at the portal. It had already turned greenish-red and everyone could hear chanting from the other side. She grew taller and more imposing and her eyes lit up into greenish balls of fire.

Elisabeth no longer looked sweet and innocent.

Katherine and Constansa looked at each other, stopped their fighting, and attacked Elisabeth instead. The empowered War Witch brushed Katherine casually away, but Constansa was a tougher nut to crack. Empowered by Heaven, she had some resistance against the infernal powers Elisabeth had become infused with. Elisabeth blasted Constansa with a huge ball of green fire, and while her own orange flames protected her somewhat, she was still blown straight across the cavern. Elisabeth briefly considered killing them all, decided against it, and turned to leave.

'You two are both cute and amusing,' Elisabeth said with a booming voice. 'The world would be a more boring place without you around, so I'll let you live. For now. But don't forget – I'll be back, you know!'

With her middle finger raised in salute, Elisabeth walked through the portal.

- TO BE CONTINUED -

EPILOGUE

It was the same dream as always. He was back on that mad battlefield, with
Katherine leading the charge. Even though they were charging over an old
parking lot, towards the artillery positions of the enemy, the half razed buildings
around the lot held ample firing positions. The parking lot had been turned into
a prepared kill zone, and they were being blown into itty bitty burning shreds.
The dragons that were supposed to provide air cover were fighting for their
lives against helicopter gunships. And with their air cover gone, they just had
to charge over open ground. Knights on proud warhorses, wolf riders, modified
bikes and cars – it made no difference. Everyone was getting blown to kingdom
come.

As usual, it was around the time they reached the first minefield that Michael
remembered he was dreaming and took control. Quite coincidentally, "taking
control" meant reenacting the things he had done during the real-world battle,
the nightmarish experience that he dreamed about. In real life, he had pissed
off - opened a portal and left, while his friends were being massacred. And he'd
dreamed this before, like a fucking groundhog day. If he was slow, he knew the
incendiary shells would start to land around them, and he would have to relive
the pleasant experience of his burning friends trying to come through the portal
after him – to no avail. He went through the motions to open the portal as fast
as he could, like so many times before, but this time something was wrong. The
portal wouldn't open - and as the shells exploded, he could actually feel his skin
starting to melt and burn. He'd never dreamt pain like that before.

He was woken by rough shaking, and the first thing he noticed was the door into
the bedroom being kicked in. One of the guards burst in, aiming his gun at the
bed.

'Everything good, boss? I heard you screaming and thought that Staschka finally
had the good sense to try and murder you!' Staschka was Michaels "wife" and
seemed to be so worried over him that she paid no attention to the guard's
disrespectful words.

'Bad dream,' Michael grunted. 'Really bad dream. Thanks for being alert, but you don't have to point the gun in our general direction anymore.' He waved dismissively. The guard put the gun away with a sheepish look and left the room

'Michael, honey,' Staschka said, stroking his shoulder and arm soothingly. 'That wasn't just a bad dream. You almost seemed possessed, with contortions and all! I know your nightmares. This was much worse.'

Staschka was the icing on the cake of the lucky streak he'd been having since that ill-fated battle. He had managed to worm his way into the court and confidence of a very petty king holed up in a set of old military mountain halls on the outskirts of Oslo, and had decided to make the best of the situation. Power, running water and enough food – as long as you didn't ask the cooks any questions you didn't want the answers to – were luxuries one no longer could take for granted. And it was a nice change to have the local thugs salute him instead of hunting him for food. As one of VIPs, he had decided to get himself a mistress from the slave pens. With all the STD's running rampant, his plan was to find a girl too young to have any of the diseases that would make his dick rot, become green and fall off. Then he'd groom her until she was old enough.

Staschka was the girl lucky enough to be the object of this plan. Staschka was no fool – she knew a good thing when she saw one. Michael wasn't violent, almost hygienic, and fairly good looking. A slave at the mercy of King Max of Kolsås could do a lot worse than being the personal slave of someone like Michael. As he had chosen her when she was very young, they'd had a long time to get to know each other before Michael took Staschka to bed. Now that was more than ten years ago, and she was pregnant with their second child. Over the years they had grown quite fond of each other, and after Staschka had borne their first child, Michael had removed her slave collar and offered to give her whatever provisions she needed if she wanted to leave with their son. Staschka had elected to stay.

'Staschka – as always, you read me like an open book. I'm not going to lie to you – I think something very bad is about happen. I need to find out what – for all our sakes,' he said, stroking her belly.

Michael went to his study, telling Staschka that this might take a while and that no one was to disturb him. With deep worry-lines on his forehead, he started testing the energy flows with his crystals. The while turned out to be quite short –ashen-faced, he emerged from the study after only a few hours. Staschka was teaching their son, Julius, how to make improvised weapons from old household utensils, but was quick to send the boy away on an errand when she saw the look on Michael's face.

'We're fucked,' Michael said gravely as soon as Julius slammed the door behind him 'Some fool just opened a portal to Hell. And what's worse, I'm the only one known to have any knowledge of portals around here. That means anyone who cares about the opening of portals to Hell will come looking for me. Including the Church.' Staschka paled, and he sighed, placing a gentle hand on her belly bump. 'You're in no condition to travel, so we'll be sitting ducks next to an oven ready for roasting ducks'

'Can't you just open one of your portals for us?' Staschka's voice was low, but hopeful.

'Normally I could. And, sure, I can still open one. But it will do us no good, sweetheart. Portal jumping is hazardous enough for healthy adults. I have no idea what it would do to an unborn child! Or its mother. And I have absolutely no intention of finding out,' Michael said, gently caressing Staschka face. 'In any case - I'm not leaving any of you behind.'

'Y-you would stay for me? For us?'

'Yes,' Michael nodded 'There's no point in me trying to hide nearby either. Whomever comes looking for me aren't going to have any qualms using you to find me. So, I'll stay in the open and make myself easy to find.' Michael sighed. 'I'm most likely toast no matter what I do, but this way, perhaps I can spare you and Julius from the fallout.'

Staschka held him tightly, tears streaking her cheeks as she cried silently. Having made his decision, Michael felt strangely calm and detached. He saw the irony that someone like him, a magical practitioner that had made it his trademark to fuck off at the first sign of danger, would go down because he chose to do the decent thing. Only novices and fools thought that good deeds were rewarded. Either they wizened up, or they died. As an academic, Michael was curious about how, exactly, the world could go even further to Hell. Well, there was no sense being gloomy about it, he figured. If they only had a short while left, there was no point in wasting time bemoaning the inevitable.

Better to light a candle, and all that. Might as well just get ready for the worst.

And face it head on.

Want more? Go to
www.futuredarkness.com

www.ingramcontent.com/pod-product-compliance
Lightning Source LLC
Chambersburg PA
CBHW070536130626
46555CB00003B/1451